Like Mayflies in a Stream

Like Mayflies in a Stream

Shauna Roberts

HADLEY
RILLE
BOOKS

LIKE MAYFLIES IN A STREAM
Copyright © 2009 by Shauna Roberts

ISBN-13   978-0-9825140-0-9

Published by
Hadley Rille Books
PO Box 25466
Overland Park, KS 66225
USA
www.hadleyrillebooks.com
contact@hadleyrillebooks.com
Attention: Eric T. Reynolds

Cover illustration copyright © 2009 by Debbie Hughes
Cover design copyright © 2009 by Hadley Rille Books

Dedicated to the memory of my father,
Edward Arthur Roberts,
1930–2008

Acknowledgments

Many people, in small ways and large, contributed to this novel. I am particularly grateful to everyone who read part or all of earlier drafts. Their excellent comments made the book much better. These people include the members of my great critique group, Laurie Bolaños, Rosalind Green, Margaret Nichols, and Farrah Rochon, whose enthusiasm and willingness to help never lagged; Jim Young, Jude-Marie Green, Cam Parish, Dave Moore, Will Morton, Yvonne Morton, and Robin Walton of Writing Orbit of Orange County, California; and Alaina Grayson.

Dr. Jörg Faßbinder of the Bavarian State Department of Monuments and Sites, Archaeological Prospection, in Munich kindly provided information on his and others' recent research on the city he calls the "Venice of the Desert." Dr. Jonathan Pritchett of the Economics Department of Tulane University in New Orleans introduced me to the concept of "commodity money" and explained its use in a barter economy.

Other people who helped with comments or ideas include Barbara De Long, Ottilia Scherschel, Dolores Else, Noelle Greene, and Rae Ann Parker.

Special thanks to Tina Black, whose proofreading was superb.

My agent, Alaina Grayson of the Halyard Agency, deserves special mention for her enthusiasm, hard work, common sense, personal attention, and knowledge of the publishing industry.

Huge thanks to Eric T. Reynolds for believing in this book and publishing it. It was a great joy to write about a time period I love so much, and he made it possible.

My deepest gratitude to Richard L. Zettler, Associate Professor of Near Eastern Languages & Civilizations at the University of Pennsylvania in Philadelphia and Associate Curator-in-Charge, Near East Section of the University Museum, for reading and providing comments on an earlier draft of this manuscript.

The University of Pennsylvania, where I spent my undergraduate years, and its wonderful University Museum gave me a great education in the ancient Near East.

My husband, David Arthur Malueg, has supported my fiction writing in ways too many to list. He has been the best husband possible for twenty-seven years and counting.

My father, Edward Arthur Roberts, was always my number one fan, encouraging me to pursue my dreams and believing in my abilities.

All mistakes are mine alone.

Thank you, reader, for buying my book. May you enjoy your visit to the exotic and wondrous city of Uruk.

Contents

Chapter 1: Protector of Gazelles

Mesopotamia, end of the dry season
Approximately 4750 years ago

AROUND THE SHRUNKEN WATER HOLE, scrawny gazelles jockeyed for position. Two fawns, shoved aside, bleated their distress. The boy stood among them, still as stone, empty water skins hanging from sticks balanced on his shoulders, waiting for the creatures to drink their fill. He kept his sling in one hand and pebbles in the other. Ignoring the sand fleas biting him, he scanned the reeds and rushes edging the water hole for something to contribute to his family's supper—a fat rat, perhaps.

He wished the water hole had attracted some goats. Gazelles were the ancestors of his clan, and it was forbidden to eat the magic animals. His hungry stomach grumbled. The rainy season had ended early, and everywhere they'd roamed since had been drought-stricken. The band had fed more often from the carcasses of starved animals than from fresh meat and recently had disbanded, each family going its own way for the dry season. Separated, some might survive until the rains began again.

Although he was only ten or eleven summers old—with so many children, his mother could never remember—he was already taller than any man in the band but his father. Fetching water had become his chore when he grew stronger than his older brothers and sisters. He was the strongest child in the band and proud of it, proud also of his ability to move among the skittish gazelles without alarming them.

So, when a gazelle's ears flicked, he tensed and dropped the sticks of water bags from his shoulders. As one, the animals bounded away in a flash of brown and white. Behind the boy, downwind, a beast snarled its frustration.

The boy whirled, his sling ready. He ran his tongue around his dry lips as he looked into the sand-gold eyes of an aged lion.

The lion, its mane ragged, its nose crisscrossed with scars, a spear shaft sticking from its side, and its left front paw dripping blood, limped toward him. Its huge paws padded silently on the sand. The boy fired off three rocks and got three hits: nose, foot, foot. The lion jerked back, shook its still-massive head, and snarled.

The boy brandished his sling at the beast. "Take that, old lion!" he shouted, clambering up a palm. "You won't get a meal here!" He stuck his tongue out for good measure. Squinting against the glare of late afternoon sun, he scanned the horizon for the lion's wives. He saw none.

Groaning, the lion eased its hindquarters down onto the sand, then its chest, and finally its front paws. It apparently preferred to wait for him than to search for fatter prey.

The boy lobbed two more stones at the lion. Ribs ridged its back. It hadn't eaten for a while. That might explain why it hunted for itself instead of leaving the hunt to its wives.

If he waited, someone would search for him. He could stay in the tree and wait for his father to come with his flint-tipped spear. But he'd never hear the end of the jokes. Better to slay the lion and take its tooth as a trophy.

He studied the beast, taking its measure. It moaned and bent to lick its bloody paw. Something in the paw caught the light—a knife of obsidian.

Only one person in the family had a knife so fine. His father.

Fear flamed in his belly and climbed up his throat, choking him. His ragged breath and strangled whimpers drowned out every other sound. Was that *Ada*'s blood on the lion's claws?

The injured lion rolled onto its side and roared weakly. From beyond a ridge of dunes, where the family had set up camp, came an answering roar.

The hair on the back of his neck stood up. His family was in danger. He edged down the tree. The lion watched him and struggled to rise, but it seemed unable to put weight on its injured foot. It slumped again to the sand.

The boy dropped and ran. Sweat streamed down his face and body in the summer heat, and his chest burned as he gasped. He pushed himself on, fighting for each breath. He neared the dune in whose shadow the camp lay. Above circled a vulture.

Exhaustion and fear fought to claim him. He refused. He forced his wobbling legs on until he reached camp and collapsed at its edge, vomiting. Sand and sky jerked around him as he lay there, his head throbbing and his now-dry skin reddening.

He had the heat sickness. He needed water, rest, cool shade. Instead, he crawled across the burning sand.

The first body he found was *Ada*'s.

Next to him sprawled a dead lioness, three spears—his father's spears—through its throat. Tears welled in the boy's eyes. His father had fought bravely. He crawled faster, croaking out for *Ama* and his brothers and sisters. Only the wind answered.

By the fire pit lay the bloodied bodies of his family and another dead lioness, vultures already picking at their flesh.

The boy pulled at his hair and shouted his grief and rage, then flailed at the feasting vultures with his fists, shouting until they flew away, their reddened heads mocking him. Once the bodies were safe, he crawled from one to another, putting his ear to the mouth of each, hoping to hear breath. But all had gone Below to join the shadows, leaving only husks.

The two nanny goats were missing. He could guess their fates: Leading away from camp were drag marks in the sand, blood-filled.

He found a water sack, untied the leather strip holding it shut, and gulped. He slung the water sack over his shoulder, then dragged himself to his mother's body. He clasped her hand and cried, tears running down his face and into his mouth, burning his chapped lips and leaving his mouth tasting of salt.

When his tears ran out, he rubbed his raw eyes dry. He couldn't stay with his family. The sun would soon set. He needed water and food and a safe place before the animals of the night came out to hunt.

He plodded back to the water hole, following his footsteps, too tired to lift his head. The injured lion still lived. It had dragged itself closer to the water hole, but its glazed eyes revealed it was dying. Some gazelles had already returned. The boy joined them, scooped up some water, and drank, keeping his gaze on the lion. The water did not ease his hunger, but it did slake his thirst. He filled his water sack and walked into the water hole to cool off. When he splashed, the startled gazelles jumped and shifted position, but as always tolerated his presence.

The lion slunk forward on its belly, its gaze fixed on a gazelle fawn.

"Not my family's totem!" the boy shouted. As if a lion himself, he vaulted from the water hole and shoved the fawn away as most of the animals bolted. The lion tried to spring, but its left leg gave way. It howled and landed in a sprawl, its tongue lolling.

The boy didn't hesitate. He yanked his father's knife from the beast's paw and struck it in the lion's eye, driving it deep and twisting. The lion toppled.

The boy's chest heaved with exhaustion and delayed terror. He fell trembling onto the burning sand next to the beast. His father's death was avenged. He had killed a lion and was now a man. But what was a man without a band?

After catching his breath, he hacked at the lion's lower jaw and cut out a fang. Later he would eat its heart.

The boy returned to the water hole. He dashed water on himself with his cupped hands and dunked his head to get rid of the lion's gore and stench.

The fawn he had saved now suckled vigorously from its mother's udder. The boy's stomach clenched. The doe eyed him as if she saw his hunger and knew her fawn would satisfy it. The boy moved toward them as smoothly as a snake, sideways, slowly, his eyes gazing into the distance. When he reached the fawn, he lifted the knife, poised to strike, then paused. What was he doing, thinking of killing his family's totem?

He slumped to the sand and rested his head on his knees. He could not survive without a band. Who would keep watch while he slept? Who would alert him to the desert's dangers?

He would join the gazelles.

He watched the fawn, his new brother, greedily eating. The boy knelt next to him and suckled.

Chapter 2: A Wedding and a Vow

Uruk
Fifteen years later
In the tenth year of the reign of Gilgamesh, end of the rainy season
Shamhat

BEER FLOWED LIKE THE *BURANUN* IN FLOOD SEASON. The tables set up in the cool inner courtyard for the wedding feast sagged under the weight of ten kinds of bread, mustard- and cumin-flavored sheep cheese, a soft goat cheese, dried dates and figs, and meats that would have been beyond counting if Shamhat herself had not placed the orders for them: goat and donkey from the desert; red deer, gazelle, aurochs, mountain sheep, and elephant from the mountain; lambs and kids and turtledoves obtained locally; and five kinds of dried fish from the River *Buranun*. The courtyard's newly whitewashed walls gleamed in the torchlight.

The bride's father had already anointed his daughter with sesame oil and gently nudged Nameshda, all blushing cheeks and downcast eyes, toward Shamhat's younger brother, Geshtu. Now the feast to solemnize the marriage was in full swing. At Shamhat's suggestion—for this was no time for showy weddings—Geshtu had foregone the musicians customary for marriages in their class; no banners hung from the house, and no juniper resin burned. Only oil lamps lit the banquet.

Shamhat feared the wedding feast was still too obvious. The wedding party itself sat in the mud brick–walled outside courtyard, luring the guests out from the house, whose walls were thicker than Geshtu was tall and muffled every sound. The house slave, Dabta, cheerful for once, sang hymns to An, the sky God, as he passed among the guests, filling and refilling their beer beakers. Shamhat had already twice gone among the laughing guests, whispering, warning them to be quiet. They knew the stakes, but were too happy with beer to remember.

Shamhat joined her best friend, Kirum, in the corner of the exterior courtyard, where she filled racks of silver beakers with *kashbir, kashsi,* and *ulushin.* Usually *Ama* would have brewed the beer, but she was still mourning *Ada*'s death. Kirum, a tavernkeeper, had volunteered to help *Ama* again.

As fast as Kirum could pour, Dabta and the hired servants took racks away to the guests. Shamhat made a move to help her friend, then remembered her dignity. It would not do for a priestess of Inanna, patron Goddess of Uruk, to be seen pouring beer. Inanna's high priest, Nanna-Ur-Sag, already disapproved of Shamhat's friendship with Kirum.

"You will have many new customers at your tavern after tonight, I think." Shamhat grabbed a beaker of *kashsi* for herself as a servant took another rack.

"You prefer the red beer?" Kirum wiped the sweat from her broad forehead.

"Tonight. But the sweet *kashbir* and the emmer wheat *ulushin* seem more popular among the guests."

Kirum cast a glance at the gate, bolted from the inside, and her moon-shaped face creased in worry. "Pray Inanna no more guests arrive."

Geshtu frowned as he approached. "I've taken precautions. We should have no unwanted visitors." He glanced at Nameshda, his hand tightening on his beaker.

"Brother, go, enjoy your feast." Shamhat gave him a shove, as she would have done when they were children.

Geshtu scowled at her. "You must give me the same respect you showed *Ada*, particularly in public." He took his new role as head of the household seriously, and their close relationship had frayed like old rope.

Fearsome pounding shook the tied-reed gate and gateposts, frightening the guests in the outer courtyard into silence. Geshtu clenched his fists. "I'll not open it. Nameshda is my property, not his." The gaze of every guest was on him. He looked only at his bride. "Like a gazelle she is—shy, graceful, innocent."

"Open up!" an impossibly deep voice slurred.

Geshtu reached for his knife. His new father-in-law, Nur-Ea, came forward and grabbed one arm as Shamhat took the other. Guests slid from the benches. Some boosted themselves over the mud-brick walls, the tails on their fleece skirts bobbing, while Dabta hurried the less agile toward the kitchen outbuilding.

"Nameshda is mine," Geshtu insisted.

"Do you want him to kill us all?" Nur-Ea asked. "The Gods punish as they will. We must endure."

"You 'endure' because you don't want to lose your position on the council. Nameshda hasn't sinned. She's only thirteen years old."

Nur-Ea, his face like cold, carved stone, struck Geshtu.

With a cry of triumph, King Gilgamesh pulled the gates free and tossed them over his head into the alley. He staggered into the courtyard, his massive shoulders knocking bricks out of the courtyard wall, and looked from woman to woman. His beard, usually so carefully curled and stiffened, stuck out in two tangled mats like the tusks of a wild boar. The gold bands binding his hair sat crookedly on his forehead. The guests who had not escaped knelt.

The bride screamed.

The king zeroed in on her and his eyes grew dark as the soot that lined them. "You did well, Geshtu. Your bride is not only rich but beautiful." Terror on her face, Nameshda scrambled under the table. Her father yanked her out, his face grim. Nameshda's costly linen robe was now dirty, her braid had come unwound, and her headdress of gold leaves sat askew.

Shamhat slid gracefully between the king and Nameshda. As a priestess of Inanna, she did not kneel to any but a deity, but she dipped her head and touched her thumb to her nose in greeting, then lifted her head to its most beautiful position. Only the most perfect could serve the Gods, and the temple had trained her since childhood to enhance her natural assets. Gilgamesh's glazed eyes gazed at her hungrily. Shamhat knew what he saw: shining black hair piled high and secured by strips of gold; the erotic tilt of her luminous eyes, enhanced by ground lapis lazuli; eyelashes made long and alluring with soot; and flawless skin, the color of toasted almonds, showing through her light linen robe.

Shamhat half-closed her eyes and tilted her head. "Good health to you, great king. Your presence honors us." She glided toward the broken gate.

"My holy jewel," he whispered, as he had ten years earlier. He put his huge hand against her cheek. "My clear-eyed one." The king turned as she moved until he faced the gate. "As king I must honor the head of my council of old men and his new son-in-law, brother of the most perfect representative of Inanna."

Shamhat licked her lips. "Our family, my king, holds to tradition." She tossed her head so her gold earrings would dance and glitter. "It would be my great honor to take you to Inanna's house to make an offering."

He wagged his finger at her. "Ahhhh, Shamhat. You seek to trick me." The king looked into her eyes with longing. "Drunk as I am, I know today's not New Year's Day, and so your vow of abstinence holds." He lifted his hands to block his view of her. "I, Gilgamesh, set the traditions now. Every bride is mine, if I so choose, before she is her husband's."

"But my lord king—"

His eyes hardened. "How dare you defy me, the ruler of this city?"

It took all her concentration not to wince at his roar. Gilgamesh turned toward the bride. Shamhat was losing him. "Inanna rules this city." No more seduction; now Shamhat spoke as representative of the Goddess. "What you do is an insult to Inanna. She'll punish Uruk."

"Silence, woman!" The king scanned the courtyard. "Does any man here disagree with my right? If so, wrestle me. Now. Here."

No man spoke. Gilgamesh was an arm's length taller than the tallest and had twice the shoulder breadth of the widest. He

21

swaggered forward and pulled the shaking, weeping bride from *Ama*'s arms, threw her over his shoulder, and carried her into the house.

Geshtu stood white-faced and white-knuckled, his eyes wild, as the guests left quietly through the broken gate, their eyes cast down. Kirum shook as if she were the intended victim, and Shamhat held her. When the courtyard was empty of guests, Geshtu grabbed a wooden beaker rack from Kirum and lifted it with both hands over his head. Beer poured out, staining his robe and wetting the dirt floor. "I'll kill him!"

He lurched into the house, and Shamhat and Nur-Ea grabbed him in the small entrance hall. Geshtu grimaced, struggling to pull free as Nameshda's whimpers reached them. "This is your fault, Shamhat. You didn't try hard enough to charm him."

"Who insisted on inviting so many guests?"

"Watch yourself, Shamhat. When you're in this house, you're under my authority."

"Stop bickering." Nur-Ea snapped his fingers at Dabta. "You, slave, take a *kuli* of beer to the king with our humble thanks for the honor he does us."

After Dabta left, Nur-Ea repeated his earlier words. "We must endure."

Nameshda's scream rang out. Crying, Kirum ran out of the courtyard. Geshtu squeezed his eyes shut, and Shamhat turned away from his humiliation. Her fingernails dug into her palms until they drew blood. Two houses down, a dog howled in sympathy. Only Nur-Ea seemed to have no trouble enduring.

Another scream, and another, and another, each louder and more full of fear. At last Nameshda's howls no longer held any humanity.

"He'll bring Inanna's wrath down on the city." *Ama*'s voice shook.

Shamhat put her arm around her. "I'll talk to the high priest tomorrow. Nanna-Ur-Sag will know what to do."

"That shuffling old man? He'll do nothing about my stolen property rights or our family's shame," Geshtu scoffed. "Shamhat,

22

you know the king. You can get close to him." He looked at her with an intensity she had never seen, the muscles in his face tense, and his eyes squeezing at the corners as if he shared Nameshda's pain. "Shamhat, I order you kill him."

Ama gasped, and Nur-Ea sucked in his breath. "One does not kill kings. And one does not talk about killing a king in front of the leader of his council of old men."

Shamhat shook her head. "I won't do it. Have you forgotten the saying, 'Don't drive out the powerful; don't destroy the wall of defense'? Gilgamesh's sins are the Gods' to deal with. And if I failed, Gilgamesh would punish my son. I would never risk Inanna-Ama-Mu's future at the temple of An."

Geshtu kept his gaze on Shamhat. "If you don't kill the king, I will. One way or another, the king must pay."

Chapter 3: The Sheepfold

Uruk
The next morning
Shamhat, Gilgamesh

EANNA, THE TEMPLE COMPLEX OF INANNA, Goddess of love and war, patron of the great city of Uruk, sprawled across a massive platform, safe from the flood waters that periodically inundated even a city as favored by the Gods as Uruk.

Uruk the Sheepfold, some called the city. Only a bad shepherd abused and neglected his sheep, Shamhat thought as she and the other priestesses processed with slow and measured steps to Inanna's inner sanctum, the cella. Of the hundreds of people who worked for the temple, only a few were allowed into the cella, where a statue of the Goddess stood on a dais, wearing robes of dyed linen, a horned headdress, and more gold and precious stones than even Gilgamesh owned.

The smell of myrrh wafted from the room. The servants had already left dishes, trays, jars, and basins outside. Like her subjects, Inanna woke with an appetite. The *en*-priest, Nanna-Ur-Sag, sang hymns of praise in his beautiful voice, still rich and forceful despite his age, and a *kurgarra*, a male priestess, plucked a lyre as the priestesses carried in the meal.

They prayed as they entered, careful not to topple any of the statuettes or other gifts worshippers had left for the Queen of Heaven. First they carried in the heavy, froth-topped jugs of beer and milk and poured the beer into the magnificent waist-high carved alabaster vase on the left and the milk into the vase's twin on the right.

Next came the platters of breads made from barley, emmer wheat, einkorn wheat, and spelt, which the priestesses set on the brick offering table. Then they offered the Goddess trays of fruits—whatever was ripe and always, always, figs and Dilmun dates, piled high, their skins murky, yet gleaming, like the Buranun that had watered their growth.

Inanna had a taste for flesh, and for the last course the priestesses took in roasted top-grade and second-grade meats: beef, barley-fattened mutton, milk-fed calf, lamb, goose, and duck as well as ostrich eggs.

After the meal, Shamhat remained to talk to Nanna-Ur-Sag. She approached him as he brushed the desert dust from Inanna's clothes.

"Nanna-Ur-Sag, yesterday my brother married the daughter of Nur-Ea of the king's council of old men."

Nanna-Ur-Sag picked up the corner of his robe and began burnishing the metal of the Goddess's body, the squint of his eyes in the dim room wrinkling his forehead and bare scalp. "Hmmmmm," he murmured, clearly half listening.

"Lord, it happened again. The king came to the wedding feast."

Nanna-Ur-Sag looked up, and his jaw tightened. "Inanna grows rich from offerings left by those who seek Her protection from the king." He waved at the rings and necklaces and pins on Inanna herself, covering her platform, and spilling onto the floor.

"Will She act soon to tame him?"

"The Gods act in their own time." The wrinkles on the priest's lined face deepened.

"Someone threatened to kill the king in revenge."

Nanna-Ur-Sag inhaled sharply. "Gilgamesh is Inanna's anointed king. His murder would bring Her wrath down on the city."

"If Gilgamesh isn't stopped, he'll bring destruction on us himself."

Nanna-Ur-Sag nodded. "We're caught like fish in a fisherman's net." Using Shamhat's arm to steady himself, he knelt, his joints creaking, in front of the Goddess. "Great Queen of Heaven, protect Uruk the Sheepfold! O bright Goddess of Love, protect Your sheep and your shepherd! Turn the king's thoughts to good! O dark Goddess of War, protect the black-headed people from threats within our walls."

Shamhat helped him up. He brushed dust off of his robe. "I will talk to the *nin*-priestess of An. Together, perhaps we can find a solution."

"What can I do?"

The priest smiled. "It's not for you to meddle in the affairs of Gods and kings. You are the Goddess's best scribe. Go to the sheepfold between the *Buranun* and the west wall of the city. The Goddess needs an estimate of its wool yield for the coming year."

Shamhat backed out of the chamber, bumping into a servant who was delivering another statuette of petition. The alabaster statuette's huge ivory eyes with their onyx pupils reminded her of Nameshda earlier this morning, when Shamhat had visited her brother's house. Geshtu had paced in the courtyard, plucking at his beard. Inside, Nameshda lay in bed staring at the ceiling as *Ama* mopped at the blood that dripped from between Nameshda's legs.

"She may return to clay," *Ama* had said. Shamhat glanced at Nameshda, and *Ama* shook her head. "She understands nothing. She dishonored her family and ours. Her burden is great."

Shamhat had knelt and taken the cloth from her mother. "Let me care for her while you wash and eat."

Remembering, Shamhat sighed. As she went to the scribes' room to get a new clay tablet and a stylus, she twitched with anger. She had lain with the king during three New Year's festivals, reenacting the sacred marriage of Inanna and Dumuzi to ensure the land would prosper in the coming year. The first time, ten years ago when the king was fifteen and new to his throne, had produced Inanna-Ama-Mu, who now trained to be a priest in the temple of An. "Inanna, Queen of Heaven, help me. Let me not hate the father of my son. Keep me from the road of sin."

But after she passed barley storerooms and neared an entrance to the temple complex, she heard the king's bellow and the cries of the sons and daughters of Uruk.

Her stylus snapped.

*   *   *

"Run, potter, run! Whoever reaches the gate of the temple of An first wins." Gilgamesh slapped the sturdy young man on the back. "I'll give you a head start of half-sixty sheep." He counted slowly, watching the man lurch and weave through the twisted alley, the tail on the back of his skirt bobbing.

Gilgamesh shouted "thirty sheep!" and bounded forward like a lion. Power surged through his calves and thighs and arms as he pumped them, the bulk and strength of his muscles like those of a wild bull aurochs. His feet touched the dirt street only long enough to spring off again. He tipped his head and bellowed his joy. He wore only a loincloth, and the humid air from the *Buranun* quickly coated his naked chest and back with a cooling film of sweat.

The windowless mud-brick walls on either side blurred. An's temple reached higher and higher to the heavens as he neared it. Wanting to push himself to the limit, he quickened his pace until his lungs burned. When he reached the temple gate, he could not bear to stop. He ran inside and leapt up the stairs to the next level, scattering priests, and then ran down again. At a time like this, life was almost perfect.

Almost. He stood at the temple gate, his hands on his hips. The potter hadn't arrived. Gilgamesh trotted back the way he had come until he found the man huffing and puffing.

The potter looked at him with obvious relief. He stopped. "You won, my lord! You are the mightiest king of all the cities."

"Don't stop now. You haven't reached the temple." Gilgamesh gave him a shove toward An's temple and matched his pace until the potter fell to his knees.

"Please, my lord." He bowed several times, his face red and shiny like a pomegranate aril. "No more! I concede defeat."

"Get up." Gilgamesh folded his arms and glared at the man.

The man tried, then fell again. He scanned the spectators. "Lugal-Ki-Ag! Send for my brothers to help me home." Lugal-Ki-Ag nodded and ran off.

Gilgamesh glowered. "Who will finish the race for the weak potter?"

People withdrew into doorways and alleys. Only one old woman with a twisted neck stood her ground.

Gilgamesh chuckled. "Grandmother, do you want to race me?"

She hobbled closer to him, leaning on a thick reed. "No, Lord King. I ask a boon."

Euphoria made him giddy. "Name it, and it's yours."

Her lips trembled more than her body. "Yesterday you gave my grandson the honor of wrestling you by the baths in the Eanna. He broke his arm and can't work. I ask, Lord King, that you send a physician to tend to him."

Uruk's sons were weaklings, all of them. "What work does he do?"

"He is a smith for your great house, Lord King."

"It shall be done."

As the woman thanked him in the name of several Gods and asked each to bless him, other women stepped forward, some crying, some hard-eyed, some with beseeching hands, some with fists propped on their hips.

"My son! You wrestled him too. Now he has no feeling in his legs and can't stand."

"My husband! You challenged him to a donkey race. He fell off and hasn't recognized me since."

Other women talked on top of each other. "My brother—" "My father—" "My son—" "My nephew—"

"Enough!" He turned and raced to An's complex. He ran in and up the stairs to the top, where the White Temple sat, plastered with white gypsum and gleaming in the sun. He paced and looked out over the huge city, his city, surrounded by walls he had strengthened and crisscrossed by streets and canals he kept in good repair. These things no one appreciated.

Where were those worthy of him? Seventy thousand men, women, and children, but not a one could match him in strength or endurance. None could match him in bravery or daring; none in size or beauty. In Uruk, he alone glowed with vitality like a beacon fire in the night. He was as lonely and bored as if the city had been abandoned to jackals.

Enlilla, the *nin*-priestess of An, approached, leaning against the wind, which blew like a winter storm here on the tallest building in Uruk. The priestess was ancient, at least forty, but age had given her features dignity. She folded her hands with calm serenity. How he envied her!

"You look troubled." She walked alongside him, the tip of her head below his armpit.

"My *zi* is stormy and restless. I can't sit still; I can't sleep. I must always be moving, always challenging people, always besting them. Why am I unsatisfied? Why can I find no equal?"

Enlilla snorted. "What do you expect? You're the shepherd, and the citizens are sheep. Lay aside your discontent. Remember the old saying, 'Accept your lot and make your mother happy.'"

"The rest of the saying is, 'Run fast and make your God happy,'" Gilgamesh reminded her.

"You've run enough to make Utu happy forever," she snapped. "Now it's time to care tenderly for your flock. Love your wife. Play with your children. These things, not games and contests of strength, give meaning to life."

She was only a woman. She didn't understand the needs of a man like him. "I so long for. . . ." He stopped and gazed out at the baked-brick city walls, gleaming in the sunlight like copper, and shook his head. "I don't know what I long for. Something's missing. Even though I am king of all I can see, I can't find what will complete me."

Chapter 4: Thief

The wilderness
Two days later
Zaidu

Z AIDU THE TRAPPER STRODE TOWARD THE WATER HOLE,
squinting against the early morning glare, his gaze raking
everything between him and the horizon for danger. He
sniffed, but smelled only rustling plants, fresh water, and dung left by
visiting animals. Birds squawked and twittered.

He adjusted the bow and quiver slung over his shoulder and
scratched at fleas under the gazelle skin he wore. The quiver hung
heavy with extra arrows, and he carried a sling and a bag of stones. He
didn't usually make his rounds of traps so armed.

But usually no one stole from his traps.

He'd gone hungry the past two days because his traps had been
empty for a week, and he had netted only a few small birds. He had
given *Ada* the last of their food and was too proud to beg the nearby
shepherds for handouts. He and *Ada* now had no hides, meat, or
horns to trade for necessities.

The previous evening, at the edge of the waterhole, he had dug a
pit and set out several small reed traps. He yearned for a good-sized
gazelle for his dinner, but would be happy with a gecko. Today he
hoped to kill the animal that stole from his traps.

He hid among the reeds, strung his bow, and waited. The sun
rose until it blazed directly above. Snipes bobbed as they thrust their
long bills deep into the wet sand and plucked them out again. A shrike
dove past his face to snatch a lizard, and a mantis skittered over his foot.

He grew drowsy in the midafternoon heat and nodded off. He woke with a jerk when something heavy crashed through his pit trap. His stomach grumbled, and he longed to check the pit to see what he would eat that evening. But he stayed put, waiting for the thief.

An unfamiliar cry shattered the air. The hair stood up on Zaidu's arms. It came not from the trapped animal, but another creature, above ground. Plants rustled; water splashed; dried reeds split with a crack. Zaidu groaned inside. The creature had destroyed one of his traps.

Curiosity and anger won out over caution. Zaidu leaned out of his hiding place.

A beast jumped into the pit. The pit was deeper than Zaidu was tall, yet half of the dark, shaggy creature was above ground. It stood on its hind legs, but Zaidu couldn't see what it did. He crawled toward it, careful to stay behind the rushes and make no sound. The beast itself hummed; it sounded almost like a mother comforting a baby. Zaidu pulled an arrow from his quiver and nocked his bow.

Still on its hind legs, the creature leaped from the pit. Cradled in its front legs was a gazelle, still alive. Zaidu readied his shot. Then the creature turned. Zaidu's heart pounded, and his limbs shook.

The thief was a demon from the Netherworld.

Zaidu didn't bother getting his shovel. He ran for his life.

"You ran away. You didn't get a good look." *Ada* rubbed his skinny arms. Since he'd gone blind and couldn't hunt, his muscles had gotten stringy, and he chilled easily.

"It was a demon. I'm sure." Zaidu put more dried dung cakes on the fire. It would keep them warm and scare away animals, but they had nothing to cook on it.

"Foolish boy, why would a demon steal from your traps? The city is full of food."

A good son didn't argue with his father. Zaidu let the insult slide and scooted closer to the fire, ignoring his cramping belly. He reached for some reeds to build a new trap.

Ada continued. "What makes you think it was a demon?"

"It stood upright and had a face like a man. Eyebrows, nose, lips."

"Bah. Plants blocked your view. You saw a bear."

Zaidu crossed two short reeds and wrapped a palm leaf stalk around the joint. "What's a bear?"

"A big animal with dark fur that lives between the rivers. It sometimes walks on its hind legs. I saw them when I used to travel to the city to trade."

"Why would a bear be here if it lives by rivers?" Zaidu shook his head and picked up the next reed. It was straight and evenly thick, so he set it aside to make a flute. "We should move our camp."

"You're overreacting. Tomorrow, kill the bear. We can sell its teeth and claws for a good price, and its pelt will make a warm blanket for winter."

The next morning, Zaidu went at dawn to visit the shepherds. Although they and their flock used the waterhole, they hadn't seen the bear his father had described. He next went to the waterhole and checked his traps.

The reed cover on the pit was gone, and so was the pit; it had been filled in. Zaidu's copper shovelhead lay where the pit had been, the wooden handle broken into several pieces. Zaidu hit his fist against his palm. That shovel had cost him twelve antelope pelts and two bone flutes. Now he would have to search for a reed of the right size, attach it to the shovelhead, and dig the pit out again.

He checked the small traps. Each lay crumpled and flat as if a giant foot had stomped on it. He set the new trap, and after filling his water skin, he scaled a palm tree to have a good view of the waterhole and the surrounding desert.

Today he had no chance to doze. A herd of gazelles bounced into view. Something two-legged ran with the herd, graceless and bulky but keeping up with the swift, lithe gazelles. Zaidu shielded his eyes against the sun and squinted. It was the same creature he had seen the day before, the one that broke his traps.

Zaidu froze. Any motion might give away his location. His heart hammered harder than before, and he felt dizzy. His enemy was strong enough to lift a gazelle and ran fast enough to keep up with one. The herd arrived, snorting and pawing, and all dipped their heads to the water and drank. Zaidu studied the creature and decided his father was right. Surely a demon would drink like a human, not like an animal. It must be a bear after all.

After drinking, the bear picked up the trap Zaidu had put out earlier and examined it, turning it with hands that looked human, despite their size and furriness. Zaidu reached for an arrow. He must have made a noise, for the gazelles bolted.

The bear shouted, lifted the trap over its head, and threw it at Zaidu. Zaidu had no choice but to slide down the tree to avoid being hit and got a good look at last at the creature.

It was no bear. It was a man. Naked, its hair uncombed and hanging to its waist, its fingernails and toenails long and yellow like claws, as much taller than Zaidu as Zaidu was taller than a child, but a man even so.

The man-creature shook his fist at Zaidu and jabbered. Zaidu could not understand the words, but he got the message: Stay away. Then the beast trotted after the gazelles.

Zaidu picked up reeds and the shovelhead and went back to their tent. Adapa the shepherd was there. He had brought *Ada* some milk to keep him strong.

"Good health to you, Zaidu." The shepherd grinned wickedly. "How many demons did you catch today?"

Zaidu was in no mood for Adapa's jokes. "The creature that's been stealing from my traps is a giant. You won't think it's so funny when he starts taking your sheep."

"He won't. We're not afraid to fight him."

Zaidu would not let a shepherd get away with calling him a coward. He looked Adapa straight in the eyes, challenging him. Adapa dropped his gaze.

"Zaidu, come in the tent," *Ada* called. Adapa loped off, and Zaidu knelt at *Ada*'s feet. "If your thief is a man, then you cannot kill him like an animal," *Ada* said. "You would displease the spirits."

"There are other water holes. Let's move our camp."

Ada drew lines in the sand with a reed. "I can't. My chest hurts too much."

Zaidu rocked back onto his heels in surprise and worry. *Ada* never complained about his blindness or other ailments. For him to admit pain meant it was bad. Zaidu would not press him again about moving camp. "What can we do?"

Ada's white-filmed eyes stared straight ahead. "Go to the city and see the great and wise Gilgamesh, the king of the black-headed people. He will know what to do."

"Which city?"

A soft smile touched *Ada*'s lips. He had fond memories of trading in the cities along the river. *Ada* had met Zaidu's mother in one and brought her to the desert, but the city woman had not been hardy enough to survive.

"There's only one city so great it needs no name," *Ada* said. "Uruk."

Chapter 5: Two Dreams

Uruk
The next morning
Shamhat, Gilgamesh

KNEELING ON A MAT OF WOVEN REEDS in the scribes' workroom, Shamhat kneaded the slick clay, adding a little water to make it softer and keep it moist. She dug the heel of her hand into it, thrusting it hard against the polished limestone slab on the low table, then folded the top toward her, turned it slightly, and repeated the sequence. The repetitive, even rhythm had become second nature to her hands, and her thoughts could wander as they would. Today, she thought again of Nameshda, who still hadn't recovered from her injuries.

Shamhat had stolen time from her temple duties the previous night to visit her brother's house. Two physicians had argued in the bedroom, and Geshtu had ranted to her about the king as *Ama* tried to hush his traitorous words. No one had noticed her. Shamhat had come back to the temple and the solace of her work with fear twisting her guts.

When the clay had an even consistency and slipperiness, she rolled it into a ball and then flattened it against the table with her palm, nudging it into a squarish shape. She picked up a reed from her pile and sliced off the edge with a knife.

Beginning was always the hard part. In her scribal records, she made a simple accounting of what was. Lambs, sixty minus three. Goatskins, twice sixty plus eight. Barley, ten *gur*-cubes. Thoughts were harder to capture.

She lightly pressed the stylus to clay, once, twice, thrice, turning slightly each time so that she made a six-pointed star. To the left she made the deeper sign for Inanna, a reed post. She continued slowly, thinking between signs, saying each syllable aloud as she made it, ignoring the other scribes as they did likewise.

"Ah, here you are, Shamhat." Nanna-Ur-Sag shuffled in the door. "Is that the record of the barley received this month?"

Shamhat stood and handed him the clay tablet. "It's another hymn."

Nanna-Ur-Sag held it from the bottom to avoid smearing the signs and slowly sounded out the words.

"Holy Inanna, fierce Goddess, Who rides into battle with roars of joy,

"May Your arrows pierce the wicked.

"Glorious Inanna, Goddess of love Who ensures fertility,

"May You comfort the violated brides, may You restore honor to their—"

Nanna-Ur-Sag bobbed his head. "A good start. How is your brother's wife?"

"No better. The physicians argue over her care."

"Put two physicians together, and you'll get three opinions. I'll pray to Bau to heal her and to Inanna to protect her." He set the tablet down on the table, his joints creaking. "Come, walk with me."

Shamhat covered the tablet with a damp linen cloth to keep the surface from crusting, then followed the *en*-priest out of the scribes' hall. Clouds gathered for the afternoon storm. A strong breeze blew from the river, reeking of fish and tanneries. The *en*-priest led her to the nearest garden, and they sat on a bench under a fig tree.

"The Lady Inanna sent me a dream." Nanna-Ur-Sag fanned himself. "In it, fields grew heavy with barley and emmer. Farmers planned a harvest and a harvest feast. They led sixty oxen to the butcher, and their wives brewed sixty barrels of beer. Then a man appeared, towering to the skies. He trampled the fields, and he poured the beer into the river. The farmers lamented and called upon the Gods. Inanna and An took pity on them and sent a wild bull aurochs. Man and beast fought, and the aurochs vanquished the man. The aurochs then helped the farmers replant their fields and brewed more beer."

"What does it mean?"

"I'd like to hear your interpretation."

Shamhat watched the Nanna-Ur-Sag's face for confirmation as she spoke. "The farmers are the people of Uruk, serving the Gods. The man who trampled the fields and spilled the beer is King Gilgamesh." The *en*-priest made encouraging noises. "The aurochs, I think, is our rescuer, someone who can humble Gilgamesh and restore order to the city."

"Enlilla and I came to a similar conclusion."

"Why an aurochs?"

"I believe our deliverance may come in an unexpected form. We must watch and wait."

Shamhat sighed. "We have been waiting so long already." Too long for some people, like Geshtu. Shamhat feared he would do something rash, something that would disgrace her and Inanna-Ama-Mu and get Geshtu in trouble. "If our savior doesn't come soon, it may be too late."

The shrine of Ninsun, the wise and all-knowing Lady of Wild Cows, lay well away from the Eanna and the temple of An in a modest residential district, so Gilgamesh was startled and annoyed to hear drums and lyres as he approached on the path along the canal. A crowd gathered on either side of the canal by the shrine, which stood several steps above the street, and Ninsun's *en*-priest stood at the top, holding a copper bowl of burning herbs. Gliding up the canal toward the shrine was a broad boat.

So much for a quiet visit with his mother.

His height gave him an advantage over the crowd, and he could see the boat well. On either side of the canal walked two unblemished white oxen, pulling the boat. Ninsun stood inside. The priestesses had dressed Her in a red wool shawl and an ankle-length white wool skirt heavily embroidered with gold thread and inset with carnelians.

She wore a gold face with inlaid eyes of lapis and an inlaid mouth of carnelian. If She were human, Her neck would have bowed under the weight of the many necklaces of gold and crystal beads. Behind the Goddess stood his mother and seven other priestesses, singing.

"Make way!" Gilgamesh shouted. The crowd quieted and fell back as he strode to the shrine. "*En*-priest, a happy festival day to you."

The priest stepped aside. "And to you, lord king. You honor us by coming to welcome the Goddess home from Her visit with Shakan."

Gilgamesh frowned. Shakan was a minor God who watched over goats, gazelles, and wild donkeys and whose shrine had only a single room. Shakan should have visited Ninsun, not the other way around. But according to his mother, Ninsun liked to get out of the cella often. Gilgamesh shifted restlessly. Even here, even now, he wanted to break free of the crowd and run.

At last the boat reached the front of the shrine. Now came the hard part for the eight priestesses: They had to lift the platform holding the Goddess and carry it inside. Gilgamesh leapt from the shrine into the boat, making it rock and causing the youngest priestess to shriek. He squatted, picked up the platform, and rested it on his head. Let his people see the might of their king and tremble! Many in the crowd cheered as he jumped to the bank and carried Ninsun on Her platform toward the shrine.

"Who is greater than Gilgamesh?" his mother shouted.

"Gilgamesh! Gilgamesh! Gilgamesh!" the crowd chanted. His chest swelled with pride, and he lifted the platform high as he carried it in. He was the most powerful man in the most powerful city in the world, the chosen of the great Inanna.

He set Ninsun down outside Her cella and stepped into his mother's room to wait.

Ama came in after the ceremony finished, her cheeks flushed. Gilgamesh kissed her and squeezed her hands, then resumed pacing the small room. How did she stand being so confined?

Ama laid her hand on his arm. "I hear such stories of you, Gilgamesh, and you look troubled. Is that why you have come?"

"My *zi* is restless. I am so alone."

Ama's brow shot up. "How can that be? You have your wife and children, and I am a short walk away. Send a messenger for me any time, and I will come."

Gilgamesh laughed. "And will you race me in the street? Wrestle me on the riverbank? I want something more than company. And then last night I had a dream. . . ."

"Ah. So we come to it, then. Was it a true dream, one sent by the Gods?"

"I believe so. When I woke, I felt such disappointment. This world seemed bitter."

"Tell me."

"In my dream I saw a star shoot across the morning sky, glowing bright and trailing a tail of light. The star fell to my feet and became a boulder. I put my arms around the boulder and kissed and caressed it. Then I took the boulder to you."

His mother closed her eyes in thought. "What did I say?"

Gilgamesh forced out the words in a whisper. "The boulder was my second self."

Ama nodded, her eyes still closed. "Soon, you will meet the companion of your heart, a loyal friend, a mighty hero, a rock to lean on. This companion will be the opposite of you and yet will be your second self."

Her words were the same as in his dream. He couldn't breathe, and his chest felt tight. He knew in his liver this man was what he lacked but could not put a name to.

"When, *Ama*? When will this companion come?"

"Soon, my son." She opened her eyes and traced a line down his face with her finger. "You will be free of this restlessness and be the king you were meant to be, like your father."

Chapter 6: Uruk

Uzarali, a small village on the outskirts of Uruk
Several days later
Zaidu

AFTER TWO DAYS OF WALKING THROUGH THE DESERT, Zaidu reached Uruk. Sand gave way to tall plants growing in long rows outlined by narrow streams. On each plot, a bent-over man hoed. Zaidu headed toward a wall of reeds that he guessed surrounded the city, ducking low and creeping so he would not be seen. Strangers were not always welcomed in the desert; city people might have the same suspicions. He didn't want to be discovered and driven away before seeing the king.

He reached the wall of reeds and peeked through a gap. Inside, surrounded by sheep, goats, and barking dogs, stood ten huge curved-roof huts made of reeds tied together. Outside the huts, a large crowd of women busied themselves with mysterious activities. Young children crawled about on the ground, and the older ones watched goats and sheep. He sniffed, and through the stench of dung smelled bread.

There would be an opening in the wall somewhere. He crawled around the edge until he saw a gate. It stood open, but a brawny young man stood outside with a flint-bladed spear. Zaidu dropped flat and watched. At last, the guard yawned. Zaidu slithered inside when the man's eyes closed.

A king would live in the biggest hut. Whenever no one was looking, Zaidu slid from house to house, avoiding the dung that lay everywhere. When he reached the king's house, he walked in.

The woman inside shrieked and clutched the baby in her arms tighter.

Zaidu held up his hands, palms forward. "I mean you no harm. I'm Zaidu. I'm here to see King Gilgamesh."

The woman's eyes went wide with fright. She skirted the edge of the room in a half-run and then dashed by him and out the door, screaming, "Help! Help!"

Zaidu would apologize later. He needed to see the king first. "King Gilgamesh?" Zaidu called out. No one answered. Continuing to call, he walked the length of the hut, richly furnished with two chairs made of reeds and a bed, but found no one. He would have to ask one of the boys.

He walked out the door and stopped short. A group of women and boys, all holding knives or thick reeds, stood outside, their faces angry and afraid. "That's it!" The woman with the baby crouched behind the others. "That's the gazelle-man." A few men burst through the gate, holding their hoes like spears in front of them.

"Don't be such a goose. Gazelles don't carry a quiver and bow over their shoulders or a flute in their hide." A bent older woman with a single thick cluster of dark chin hairs took a hesitant step forward. "Can you understand me?" she shouted at Zaidu. "Are you here to trade?"

"I'm not a trader, honored Grandmother. I'm here to talk to King Gilgamesh."

Several women giggled, and Zaidu stood straighter. "King Gilgamesh," he repeated. "This is Uruk, right?"

"No, desert man. You're in Uzarali." The old woman pushed one of the boys forward. "Show him." The boy scampered up a contraption of tied-together reeds that rested against the hut. Zaidu watched how he did it, then awkwardly followed.

"There." The boy pointed. "That's the city. It's a day's walk from here."

Zaidu's stomach fell. The city spread out on both sides of a great river with many branches. Inside its walls a sixty sixties of buildings stood, packed together in clusters, with large spaces of green in-between. Near the center of the city stood an odd mountain with a white building on top. In such a huge place, how would he ever find King Gilgamesh?

As Zaidu's foot hit the ground, sharp objects jabbed his back. He froze, chiding himself for his rare lapse in attention. He had been too distracted by the problem of finding Gilgamesh to listen.

"What do you want here?" The voice was rough and deep. Zaidu counted the breath of six other men.

"I need to see King Gilgamesh. I thought this was Uruk." None of the men found it funny, as the women had. The first man said, "I don't believe you. Who could be that stupid?"

Slowly, Zaidu put his other foot down. Slowly, he stuck his arms out to the sides, and slowly he turned to face the men. He kept his stance relaxed and his gaze slightly down, as if he had stumbled on a dangerous animal. He swallowed to loosen his throat so his voice would come out calmly. "I guess *I* am that stupid."

This time, some of the men did laugh. "Fresh out of the desert, are you?"

"My first time. I hope my last."

The men's bodies relaxed, although the hoes and shovels continued to threaten Zaidu's chest.

"I'm Utul, the big man of Uzarali." Short but broad-shouldered, the man spoke with authority. "How did you get by our guard?"

"I'm Zaidu the trapper. My father taught me how to move so that I'm not heard or seen."

Utul flipped his spear so it pointed to the sky and nodded at Zaidu's bow. "Can you hunt as well as trap?"

Zaidu nodded.

"Then welcome to Uzarali." Utul made a sharp gesture with his hand, and the other men lowered their weapons. "We'll put you up for the night and feed you. In exchange, you'll do us a favor." His voice made it clear Zaidu had no choice in the matter. Zaidu's muscles tensed as he waited to find out what the favor would be. "We need your help to get the sheep and goats out of the village."

Zaidu raised his eyebrows. It was a simple task, one any of the older children could have done. He agreed.

But a herdsman was not what the village needed. Instead, dusk found him crouched low in the reeds by a muddy waterway the villagers called a "canal" with Dimshah, the village's largest dog, watching a sheep tethered nearby. The sheep bleated, fearful to be separated from the comfort of its flock. It would have been more afraid if it had known it was staked there as bait for a leopard. The large cat had been killing the village's livestock until the villagers had brought all the animals inside the compound. Zaidu's task: Kill the leopard.

The job was far more difficult here than it would have been in the desert. Zaidu knew the sounds and smells of his homeland. Here, new smells layered one on top of another, as did sounds—the murmur of the water, the villagers talking, and the wind rustling in the reeds and crops. They would disguise any hints of the cat's approach. So he had borrowed the dog for its keener nose and ears.

The sound of the canal changed. A regular slow swish had joined its previous erratic lapping. Zaidu looked at Dimshah. Its ears swiveled forward.

Zaidu crept through the reeds toward the sheep while fitting an arrow to his bow. One shot—one shot that killed instantly—was all he would get. Although leopards preferred sheep to people, they would eat anything they could catch, and they became a blur when they ran. A leopard angered by a painful arrow would be on him in the space of a breath.

Dimshah joined him and growled low in its throat. Zaidu didn't look for the leopard; its spots would let it blend into the reeds in the twilight. Instead, he looked at the sheep and watched for motion in the corner of his eyes.

There! He drew a deep breath to help him keep his focus on the sheep. The rank, sour smell of cat urine assaulted his nose. The sheep must have smelled it as well. It struggled to run, but succeeded only in tripping and falling, bleating loudly.

Zaidu rose, aimed where he predicted the leopard would cross, and shot. An angry scream burst from the darkness, then cut off.

Dimshah bounded forward, Zaidu close behind. The leopard lay, still and blank-eyed, an arm's length from the downed sheep, which trembled so hard Zaidu feared it would die from fright. The dog barked once and lunged forward with its back feet firmly planted; the leopard did not respond.

Zaidu had saved the village livestock.

"It's done!" he shouted toward the village. The gate opened, and men ran out with spears and a torch. Dimshah barked and jumped.

"Dead with a single arrow!" Utul looked at Zaidu with respect. "You are now a member of this village. You'll find hospitality at my home anytime."

"Come," another man said. "The women have prepared a feast of roasted goat, emmer bread, and barley and lentils."

Zaidu retrieved his arrow and slung the leopard carcass over his shoulder. "They were that certain I would survive?"

"No." Utul was as blunt as always. "But you gave the women such a laugh when you mistook our village for Uruk they prepared a feast just in case."

Humbled, Zaidu returned to the village with the men and ate a good meal for the first time since the wild man had started visiting the water hole. Afterwards, the men gathered in Utul's hut to talk and drink *kashsi* out of a large jar through reeds. Zaidu told them about the wild man and played his flute for them. They gave him instructions for making his way in Uruk, warning him about thieves and beggars and, once they were drunk, telling him where to find the best prostitutes.

Chapter 7: The Greatest City in the World

Uruk
The next day
Zaidu, Gilgamesh

FOLLOWING THE INSTRUCTIONS THE VILLAGERS HAD GIVEN him and with the help of a boy who accompanied him part way, Zaidu reached Uruk, the real one. The boy came in handy; Zaidu otherwise would have been stymied by the first of the many canals and rivulets they crossed as the land grew increasingly marshy. The guards at the gate had questioned him and then let him in, saying that he could ask anyone for directions to the king's great house.

His muscles ached, the result of so many hours spent at Uzarali on alert against danger. Uruk did not bring out the same wariness. He could see only a small part of it at once, and he pretended the building-lined paths were canyons with rock walls and the many men and pigs, wild goats.

A woman walked out a doorway and, without looking, tossed the contents of a pot onto the path. Zaidu jumped away barely in time to avoid being splattered by yellow liquid that smelled like piss and overwhelmed the sweet and comforting smell of barley that perfumed the city.

He approached a kindly looking young woman carrying a basket on her head. "Where do I find King Gilgamesh?" he asked. She looked at his gazelle skin and hastened her steps, veering around him.

"Where do I find King Gilgamesh?" he asked a man whose upper arms were encircled with bands of gold. Even though Zaidu

45

had washed in the water hole before leaving home, the man wrinkled his nose and then used his thumb and finger to pinch it shut. After several more tries, Zaidu leaned against a wall to think. A man wearing the same sash as the guards came toward him. Before Zaidu could speak, the man barked, "Move along. No loitering."

Zaidu would have to find the king's great house on his own. He walked the narrow, twisting streets. Each time he passed a street whose houses were bigger, he turned onto it. Despite his excellent sense of direction, he was soon thoroughly lost.

A short man wearing nothing but a ragged, filthy sheep fleece skirt and carrying a worn basket approached. He stank as if he had not bathed in weeks. Eyes downcast and murmuring, he shoved his basket toward Zaidu. Curious, Zaidu looked in. The basket contained two broken pieces of bread and some uncooked barley. Zaidu had not eaten since before he left Uzarali, and now someone had taken pity.

"Thank you, friend." Zaidu grabbed one of the offered breads and stuffed it in his mouth. His eyes half-closed in pleasure. The grain had been so finely ground that the bread gave way easily under his teeth, with no rocks or grit to jar his jaw.

"*Ashe!*" His benefactor's face grew indignant as he took hold of the edge of bread sticking out of Zaidu's mouth and yanked. "You're supposed to give something, not take something. Now you have to pay for the bread you stole."

Awareness dawned. This little man must be one of the beggars the villagers had warned him about. Zaidu examined him curiously, wondering how such a man could live with dignity. "I've got nothing to give you."

"Nothing?" The beggar narrowed his eyes. "You're wearing a gazelle skin and carrying a bow and a flute." The beggar reached out and rubbed the gazelle skin between his fingers. "I'll take this old skin."

Zaidu dealt with traders several times a year. He stood at last on familiar ground. "This beautiful skin, scarless and finely tanned? It's worth far more than a stale crust of bread."

The beggar picked his nose and shifted from foot to foot. "You can have the other piece of bread, too."

Zaidu swallowed the last bit of bread in his mouth. His stomach begged for more. "You can have the skin if you both give me the bread and take me to King Gilgamesh."

The beggar scratched at red fleabites along the edge of his fleece skirt and looked longingly at Zaidu's gazelle skin. "See the white building, high in the sky?"

"On a mountain?"

"That's the house of the God An. The large building between it and us is the Eanna, the house of the Goddess Inanna. King Gilgamesh lives in the Kullab district on the other side of An's temple. Once you get to the Eanna, anyone can give directions."

Zaidu already knew how likely that was. He shook his head. "You have to come with me. Otherwise, no deal."

The beggar licked his scaly lips. "Fine. But I want the skin now."

And then he'd run off, Zaidu suspected. He snatched the beggar's begging basket. The man would not be able to beg without it. "You'll get your basket back at the king's house."

"Deal."

Zaidu pulled out the bone pins that held the skin together at his shoulders and waist and held it out. Only then did he notice he alone in the crowded street wore no garment. The beggar wrapped the gazelle skin around his waist and then jerked his head toward the Eanna. "Come on. I need to get back to work."

"In the desert, we have long memories. One day I'll repay you for this favor."

The beggar snorted his disbelief.

He led Zaidu on many streets, crossing two canals and once going through a building. Zaidu could never have found his way on his own.

The beggar talked as they walked, naming the people they passed, pointing out shrines to various Gods, and giving him tips for begging because, the beggar said, "you'll not find someone as generous as me again, and you'll need to get food somehow." Zaidu welcomed the beggar's chatter as a distraction from the stares, giggles, and whispers he attracted. Other than him, only tiny children went naked, and he wished he had included the filthy fleece in the bargain.

When they reached the walls enclosing the Eanna, the beggar stopped. "Which God do you pray to?"

Zaidu named several of the spirits *Ada* had taught him. "Never heard of them." The beggar's voice was scornful. "If you need a personal God, Inanna's the best one, take my word. Uruk is her city."

Zaidu studied the colored wall of the Eanna and the tops of the tall buildings and palms behind. He had never heard of Inanna. Her house was clearly the biggest he had seen yet, though, and she had many date trees. She must be the most powerful God, even though she was only a woman. A shadow appeared at the gate as he watched.

The Goddess herself stepped out of the gate, bright and shining. People bent their heads to her, so Zaidu did as well, his heart thumping in his throat.

The Goddess did not wear a sheep fleece. She was wrapped in a shawl of the finest skin he had ever seen, so thin it folded and molded to her body as she walked, and he could see the shadows of her legs. Jewelry of gold and polished stones decorated her ears, arms, and head. Under a broad forehead her cheekbones slanted at an angle and drew attention to her full mouth. Outlined in black, her eyes outshone the full moon at midnight, and her movements were purposeful and graceful. She was a leopard in human form.

Then she apparently caught sight of them, and Zaidu held his breath. She looked him up and down, then came toward them, took off one of her earrings, and handed each a bead of silver. "For food and clothing. May Inanna bless you." Words streamed from the beggar's mouth as he knelt before her. Zaidu could only look at the Goddess in awe. She caught his eye and smiled.

It was the best moment of his life.

The public courtyard of Gilgamesh's house teemed with sweaty bodies and overflowed into the corridor. Nearly all of the council of old men had showed up for today's meeting, and many had to perch on the edge of pots holding plants or stand. Gilgamesh heard his lady wife singing to his children and wished he could join them for some games. Even better, he wished he could throw off his necklaces of gold and run through the streets as the air cooled for the night.

Instead, he shifted on his throne, cracked his knuckles, and yawned as the members took turns droning about dredging the irrigation canals. The canals always needed dredging; he always conscripted citizens as the council requested. Why did they have to natter on and on when there was nothing to debate?

He slapped his hand on the arm of his throne. "The same number of men as last year, at the same pay." He stood. Most of the council took the hint, and the members began gathering their tablets.

The guard Babati walked into the courtyard. "Lord King, a naked beggar insists on speaking with you."

"Don't disturb the king with such foolishness," Nur-Ea grumbled. "Send the wretch away."

Intrigued, Gilgamesh held up his hand and cut the leader of the council off. "Don't speak for me, Nur-Ea." He sat on his throne and smoothed his beard. "Bring the man in." He'd been waiting for the companion his dream had promised. Even if this beggar was not he, his humble circumstances combined with his cocky behavior promised a diversion.

The man walked in, tall and straight, flicked his gaze about the courtyard noting the palms and the doorways, and headed for Gilgamesh. This man was no beggar. Gilgamesh leaned forward, a leap of excitement in his chest. Though the man sported nothing but a bow and quiver over his shoulder and a flute in his hand, his trunk was pale, showing he usually wore clothes and spent much time outside. His dusty shoulders and legs bulged from hard work, and he moved purposefully and silently. He did not kneel or bow or even offer the courtesy of touching his thumb to his nose.

The man came from the wilderness. A hunter or trapper, probably. Gilgamesh took a guess. "Welcome, trapper. You have come a long way to see me."

The man's eyes flew open under his arrow-straight brows, and he took a startled step back. "You are as great and wise as my father said."

Gilgamesh snapped his finger at his *sagi*, his cupbearer. "Bring this man beer and bread and a clean fleece." Many of his council of old men gasped, and Gilgamesh smiled. Unexpected largesse was a surprisingly effective way for a king to earn loyalty. Besides, no man should go naked in his city, the greatest in the world.

"Thank you, great king," the trapper said. "I am Zaidu. I walked three days from the desert to ask your help."

"Bow to me, Zaidu. It is our custom." When the man did nothing, Nur-Ea hissed. Gilgamesh said gently, "Bend over at the waist." Zaidu obliged.

"Now tell me, why do you need my help?" Gilgamesh drummed his fingernails lightly on his throne, unable to keep still.

"Recently, my traps were empty day after day. The animals kept escaping, but I didn't know how. I hid by the water hole to find out why. The first day, something large and hairy came and let all the animals out. It had the strength of a God. It lifted a gazelle from a pit trap as easily as I could lift a baby."

"He's telling stories," Nur-Ea protested.

"I did not give you permission to speak." Gilgamesh glared, and Nur-Ea sat on the bench with a huff. "Continue, Zaidu."

"I thought it was a demon at first. But when I got a better look, I saw it was a wild man." Zaidu stopped his story to grab the *kuli* of beer the *sagi* brought in. He chugged half of it.

"A wild man who frees animals?" Gilgamesh leaned forward, keen to hear more.

"Yes. He leaves no animals for *Ada* and me to eat or trade. *Ada* is too frail to move camp. We'll starve if you can't help us." Zaidu finished the beer—even the dregs at the bottom, Gilgamesh noted with amusement—and wiped his arm across his mouth. The *sagi*, at Gilgamesh's nod, wrapped the fleece around Zaidu's waist and pinned it.

"Tell me more about this wild man."

"He is almost as tall as you, great king, and broader in the shoulders. He runs with the gazelles."

Gilgamesh himself had never raced a gazelle, but he imagined it would be a hard contest. No one in the city could match him, but this man of the wilderness might be a worthy opponent. "Is he dangerous?"

"He threatened me." Zaidu ripped the end off of a round loaf of emmer bread and stuffed it in his mouth. "But he didn't hurt me. I called him wild because he doesn't talk and wears no clothes."

Gilgamesh's mouth twitched. "You wore no clothes when you arrived, and clearly, you are no wild man."

"I gave my clothes to a beggar." The trapper ripped another piece from the loaf of bread.

"He gave away his clothes?" Nur-Ea clearly couldn't comprehend the generous gesture. "The trapper is mad."

"Yet I am inclined to help him." It was worth it just to provide an example of mercy to the hard-livered man.

"I would be grateful forever," Zaidu said. "I would praise the name of Gilgamesh to our spirits and ask them to protect you from evil."

Nur-Ea spoke again, his reddening face revealing his rising temper. "This wild man is dangerous. I advise sending your twenty best archers and ten of your guards to kill it."

Zaidu seemed offended. "If I wanted him dead, I'd have killed him myself. But killing a man would make me a murderer."

"Well spoken, Zaidu." Gilgamesh took a sip of his beer to hide his elation. "I want this wild man captured and brought to me." The wild man was his match in strength and size. He was the companion of his heart, he had to be.

The council members murmured. Nur-Ea approached the throne. "Sending a large contingent of men would still be best. My oldest son would be a good choice to lead them."

"This is a time for diplomacy, not force." Gilgamesh stood, sick of putting up with their denseness. He named the single person he would send.

The council of old men looked at him with varying expressions of shock, except for the eldest of all, who dozed peacefully in the shade of a potted palm. Nur-Ea pressed his lips together, apparently taking the decision as insult to his son.

"Why are you so surprised?" Gilgamesh shook his head in exasperation. "My guards are brave, but this is not a job for fighters. The wild man needs taming. Who better to gentle him and entice him to the city?"

Chapter 8: Clash of Two Cultures

"THERE'S THE BEGGAR." Zaidu pointed to the man wearing his gazelle skin. The servant King Gilgamesh had lent him eyed the beggar with contempt and held tighter to the basket of supplies. Zaidu walked over to the beggar, who with downcast eyes shoved his begging basket in front of him. Zaidu reached in and took a piece of bread.

"Why you—oh!" The beggar looked Zaidu and the borrowed servant over and smiled. "You've come up in the world in a short time, my good friend. That's a fine fleece you're wearing and a fine servant carrying your things. Surely you can spare some silver for the one person who helped you when you arrived."

"I don't like having a tail. I'll gladly trade you this skirt and some silver for my gazelle skin."

The beggar beamed. "With pleasure."

Zaidu unpinned his skirt and let it drop. "Wait!" the servant said, flustered. "Not here. Go in an alley."

Zaidu ignored him, and the beggar removed the gazelle skin. The servant stood between Zaidu and some female passersby, who giggled and stretched their necks to see around him. Zaidu put his skin on, glad to be out of the skirt. The gazelle skin had more dignity and displayed his status as a trapper.

The beggar did not dress but beat the clean fleece against the wall and then threw it into a puddle of urine at the edge of the path and stomped on it. He then wrapped it around him over the filthy skirt he already wore. He grinned at Zaidu. "A good lesson to learn, if you ever turn beggar. People are more likely to feel sorry for you if you dress and smell worse than them."

Uruk was a stranger place than he ever could have imagined. Zaidu reached into the basket the servant carried and took out a loaf of bread and a ring of silver and dropped them in the beggar's basket. "My debt is repaid."

As the beggar babbled his thanks, the servant jerked on Zaidu's arm, clearly impatient. "We must hurry." Zaidu pulled away, disgusted. The rude servant would not survive long in the desert. Zaidu often sat in one place for half the day with his snare waiting for birds. The servant huffed. "We need to reach the Eanna before they start Inanna's first evening meal."

"To the Eanna?" That was where Zaidu had seen the Goddess. His mouth got as dry as the time he and the shepherds had hunted a vicious pack of wolves that preyed on the flock. Perhaps he would see the Goddess again. "The fellow who'll tame the wild man is at the temple?"

The servant smirked. "Not quite." He strutted pompously onward. Zaidu followed, zigzagging around the many people who parted for the king's servant but not for him. Soon they arrived at the high wall Zaidu had seen before. The servant motioned impatiently for him to go through the gate.

Zaidu did and stopped in astonishment. He did not have words for what he saw. More date palms stood in a cluster than he had seen in his whole life. Within a fence stood some sheep with fuzz instead of hair and too-short horns. Scattered among the massive buildings before him stood trees and shrubs, some covered with flowers. One building rose high enough to pierce the heavens.

The servant quickened, calling, "Come on." Zaidu sprinted to catch up. The servant led him to the entrance of a building.

A beautiful woman greeted them. "I come from the king with urgent news for Nanna-Ur-Sag and Shamhat," the servant said.

"I'll get them."

The servant shoved the basket of Zaidu's supplies into his arms. Zaidu looked around and behind him. The walls outside had been the color of clay. Inside, the walls were white. People came and went, carrying baskets, jars, huge platters of food, clay molded into the shape of people, and things he could not identify.

A small figure approached from the gloomy interior. This must be Shamhat, the man the king would send with him. Zaidu squinted into the darkness, disappointed. Shamhat was slight, not the warrior Zaidu expected. "The *en*-priest will be here soon," Shamhat said.

Zaidu started. Shamhat was a boy. He had an unusual voice, soft and lilting like a woman's but strong like an adult's, without any hint of breaking.

"Good evening, Lady Shamhat." The king's servant said, touching his thumb to his nose.

A jolt of alarm broke Zaidu's calm. Shamhat was a woman? He could not take a city woman into the wilderness. Women were weak in body and mind and *zi*, and city women were especially fragile. No, this was impossible.

The woman Shamhat stepped into the light. Zaidu dropped the basket. Before him, shining with gold and sparkling with jewels, stood the beauty he had seen that morning. The Goddess Inanna.

The king had sent her a straight-browed nomad dressed in a gazelle skin.

Shamhat studied the nomad from under her lowered lashes as Nanna-Ur-Sag and Gilgamesh's servant discussed the king's order. The king wanted her to go to the wilderness to tame a wild man who had destroyed the nomad's traps. She narrowed her eyes. Because of her beauty and training at the temple of Inanna, she could tame any man. The nomad himself was clearly infatuated with her already.

Why hadn't he taken care of the wild man himself? She could read men, and this nomad was not someone easily intimidated. His body lacked the fat of a city man, to the point he looked as hard and sculpted as a statue. Scars crisscrossed his arms and legs. He had walked three days barefooted to do the unthinkable: Ask a favor of the world's greatest king. If the nomad—Zaidu—couldn't control the wild man, she herself should be wary.

"Please excuse us," Nanna-Ur-Sag said. He led Shamhat to a nook out of hearing range.

Zaidu followed. Shamhat turned to him. "'Please excuse us' means we wish to talk alone." She kept her voice gentle and whispered so the contemptuous servant would not hear her correct Zaidu, but the trapper's face hardened anyway. Ah, a proud man. Making no noise as he strode with confidence, Zaidu returned to wait with the servant. She couldn't help but watch.

"I believe this is the opportunity my dream promised," the *en*-priest whispered. "The Gods have sent this wild man to tame Gilgamesh."

Shamhat's mouth grew dry. "For the city's sake, I hope so."

Nanna-Ur-Sag put his hand on her tense shoulder, his face tight with worry. "I'd send the temple's strongest workers with you, but the king wants you to go alone."

"If Inanna sent him to be our champion, She will guide me and protect me." Shamhat dared to look into the *en*-priest's eyes for confirmation, but found none.

"What if my dream was a false one?" he fretted. "To send you on such a dangerous journey alone with this trapper would be a sin." Nanna-Ur-Sag's right eye spasmed under its thin eyebrow. "I'm going to refuse the king."

His words didn't relieve her anxiety. "What if Inanna sends no one else? I admit, I don't want to go to the wilderness. But Gilgamesh must be checked." Or else her brother would do something rash.

The *en*-priest's face grew more distressed. "You may have to break your sacred vow of chastity to tame the wild man. I may have to punish you when you return."

Shamhat looked down at her clenched hands. Lusty men and fierce animals frightened her less than the thought of being demoted or cast out of the sisterhood of priestesses. She had come to live at the temple when she was twelve, when the promise of her future beauty appeared. Like all the priestess, she enjoyed her high status. But she also loved the rhythm of the daily round of rituals. She wanted no life but that of a priestess.

She pressed the matter anyway. "The Goddess requires Her priestesses to be chaste. Yet She also requires us to learn to carry ourselves like Goddesses, to paint our faces, to style our hair, to scent ourselves, to entice men with glances and postures and words. Now She needs me to tame a wild man, and I have the skills to carry out Her desires."

"Inanna gave us rules," Nanna-Ur-Sag fussed. "We shouldn't break them." He bobbed his chin. "That's my final decision."

So her chastity—and her position—remained safe. Shamhat dipped her head in acquiescence and followed the *en*-priest to the waiting men.

Nanna-Ur-Sag addressed the servant. "Tell the king I have sympathy for the trapper's plight, but I won't let my best scribe go into the wilderness for a whim."

The servant raised his nose higher in the air. "The king has taken Inanna-Ama-Mu from the temple of An." Shamhat's hand flew to her chest, and the servant's mouth twisted into a cruel smile. "If you don't comply with the king's wishes, he will transfer responsibility for distribution of barley to the temple of An, and Shamhat will never see Inanna-Ama-Mu again."

Chapter 9: The Descent

Uruk and Uzarali
Early the next morning
Shamhat

AS SHE WAITED AT THE TEMPLE'S GATE, Shamhat rummaged through her basket for the fifth time. She had packed quickly, guessing what she might need. Bread, beer, and dried dates, of course. A flask of clear water. The necessities of her station: cosmetics, jewelry, scented oil, robes, and shawls. Small bags, filled with barley, to buy things. And of course, pomegranates and wool to prevent the wild man's seed from taking root in her womb.

"Are you ready to leave, daughter?" The ancient *en*-priest moved toward her with his usual calm shuffle, but the tightness of his face gave away his nervousness.

Shamhat smiled tightly. She had visited her brother and *Ama* to let them know of her journey and begged Geshtu on her knees not to act yet against the king. She had visited Kirum to say goodbye and get some skins of beer.

"This is to protect you in the wilderness." Nanna-Ur-Sag held out, as if presenting it to Inanna Herself, a long dagger and a sheath. "I also placed a statuette before the Goddess on your behalf."

Shamhat shivered at the danger he implied. She took the items and threaded her sash through the slits on the sheath. "I'll do what I must to save the city and my son," she vowed.

"Before you leave these gates, give me your headdress." The *en*-priest's distress showed in his jerky movements and averted gaze. "You're an agent of the king's now, not of the temple."

Her headdress was part of who she was, a priestess. Shamhat shook her head, but Nanna-Ur-Sag kept his hands out. At last Shamhat removed her headdress with shaking hands and gave it to him. Her hair unrolled and fell down her back. Fighting an absurd urge to cry, she walked out of the gate.

She took a boat from the White Quay to the north city gates, where Zaidu would meet her. Even without her headdress, most of the people recognized her as a priestess and put their thumbs to their noses in greeting.

Zaidu was waiting when she arrived. He looked at her with cow eyes until she got close, then he frowned with disapproval. "The little rocks around your neck are too tight. Something could catch them and choke you. Take them off."

She always wore these lapis lazuli beads, a sign of her high status. "I'm a priestess of Inanna, the Queen of Heaven, and you are nobody. I wear what the Goddess wishes, and *you* will follow *my* orders."

He had the impertinence to look her in the eye. "In the desert, I'll be the man who keeps you alive. Do as I say."

People stopped talking and gawked at the spectacle of a rustic chastising a priestess. Shamhat had to maintain her dignity and rank. "Follow me," she ordered and walked out the gate without a glance back.

"Lady of Inanna!" A guard ran after her. "Forgive me for listening. I've been to the wilderness. It's a terrible and dangerous place. If you wish to give me your necklace, I'll take it to Lord Nanna-Ur-Sag for safekeeping."

"You advise me to follow the wishes of a *trapper*?"

The guard paled. "You're wise in the ways of the city. The trapper knows the ways of the desert. Please let him protect you."

The guard was right. Shamhat reluctantly untied the thin sinew on which the beads were strung and handed them to the guard. "May Inanna keep you from sin." At least she still wore two strands of shell beads and her cylinder seal with its carved scene of Inanna at a banquet. Her head high, she walked to a wide canal that carried the life-giving waters of the *Buranun* to villages and fields outside Uruk. She surveyed the handful of tanned, squinty men who waited with their long pitch-covered boats and chose the man with the best-maintained craft.

"We wish to go into the desert. Sail us to where we need to start our walk."

The boatman held out his hand.

She gave him a stern look. "I may not wear my headdress and beads, but I am a priestess of Inanna."

"I know, my lady, but that one isn't." He nodded his head toward Zaidu.

Sighing, she fished in her basket for a bag of barley. The boatman shook his head. "I've got business upstream in Sippar. I'll take your shell necklaces."

"I'll take another boat, then." But when she went to the other boatmen in turn, each wanted an outrageous amount of barley, enough to buy several new shell necklaces. Reluctantly, Shamhat took off the two strands of shell beads she wore and handed them to the original boatman. He helped her and Zaidu into the boat.

The boatman paddled silently, and the craft slid through water dark with nourishment for the land. Sunlight glared off its surface, and Shamhat shaded her eyes with her hands. Both she and Zaidu craned their necks to look around. This border between civilization and wilderness must be as strange to Zaidu as it was to her. Small canals split off from the main one at regular intervals, separating long green fields of barley and wheat. The water lapped against the sides of the boat and Zaidu played his flute, lulling Shamhat into a doze.

When she woke, they floated on a minor canal. Dark shapes rustled in the reeds, willows, and licorice growing wild on the levees. The day's heat increased as the sun rose to its highest point. Bare-chested workers in the fields wiped their foreheads and bald scalps. Shamhat fought the urge to do the same. Sweat trickled down her face and her back under her heavy hair. She touched a finger to her cheek; it came away streaked with soot and powdered lapis.

She humiliated the Goddess, looking like this. When the boatman at last drew up to a small reed dock at the canal's end, Zaidu climbed out and without a word began cutting reeds. Shamhat wished the boatman good health, then climbed out and knelt by the canal and dashed water on her face. It took several rinsings before her reflection looked clean. She dried her face off with the bottom of her robe. She had done nothing yet but ride in the boat, and the garment was already dirty with dust and water splashes. Wiping her face added streaks of blue and black.

She checked her reflection again in the rolling water. She no longer looked like a priestess, only a noblewoman. If Inanna had not chosen her, this woman was who she would be, an aging, uneducated woman at the beck and call of a man. Her stomach knotted and she turned away.

Zaidu strode away, reeds under his arm, and she scurried after him, holding up her skirt, aware of how undignified she must look and chagrined by it. They must be near the edge of the outermost fields. Barren areas alternated with green fields, and they passed a herd of wild reddish-brown mouflons, their straight hair and heavy horns making them look more like goats than sheep. Despite the heat, a chill went up her arms. Civilization's end was near. Soon there would be nothing but bare desert and wild beasts. "Do you know where to go from here?"

"Uzarali."

"Do you always talk so little?"

"Do you always babble?"

Shamhat gritted her teeth and gave up her attempts at polite conversation. They came to a village surrounded by a palisade of reeds. Zaidu sped his steps and went in ahead of her. As priestess, she should have entered the gate first. She clenched her jaw. The wild man was not the only one she would have to teach the ways of civilization.

Dogs barked, and children came running. "Zaidu! Zaidu!" they cried as dogs rolled on his feet. The largest dog of all came to her, its ears back, the coarse dark hair on its scruff erect, and its pink lips stretched to reveal large teeth. It barred her way.

A man came out of the nearest house, a flimsy reed shack like the homes in the poorest areas of Uruk, and shouted at the dog. "Dimshah! Be quiet!" Dimshah whined and kept suspicious eyes on Shamhat.

Other villagers gathered. "Did you see King Gilgamesh?" "Was he as tall as a house and as strong as an ox?" "Did the king give you a wife?" "Will you stay the night?" Children hung on his legs.

Zaidu held up his hands. "I met with the king. He is a mighty man, handsome and strong and tall. He gave me gifts and bade this priestess of the great Goddess Inanna to work magic on the wild man."

No wonder Zaidu had not protested receiving one small woman to conquer his enemy. He thought she had the powers of the Goddess. She did not correct him.

"I welcome your invitation to stay, and I'll make you several traps in thanks." He dropped the reeds next to the gate.

A farmer grabbed Dimshah by its scruff and pulled the dog away from the gate, but not far enough for Shamhat to enter. "How will you repay our hospitality?" he asked. Apparently the enthusiastic welcome Zaidu received didn't extend to her. She held out three bags of barley, but he didn't take them. "Didn't you see the fields? We have plenty of barley almost ready to harvest." The farmer's gaze fastened greedily on the crystal cylinder seal with gold findings hanging about her neck. She rummaged in her bag and pulled out a silver ring. Surely he wouldn't turn down such a wealth of silver.

He did.

She put her hand over her seal. No one of any consequence went about without a seal, let alone a priestess. She shook her head. The farmer continued to block her way.

She wouldn't need to put her mark on documents out here. With a sigh, she pulled the chain holding the cylinder seal off. "If you sign any contracts with my seal, I'll take you to court," she warned.

He grinned. "No courts out here." He stepped aside so she could enter.

She sucked in her breath. The tiny village had no streets, and the ramshackle huts showed no plan or organization. Dust and dung lay everywhere, and flies buzzed about.

Shamhat squared her shoulders and lifted her chin. She could not let the squalor bother her. She was a priestess.

Besides, things would be worse when they entered wasteland the next day.

* * *

The next morning, Shamhat ate her lentils and barley bread as quickly as was polite, eager for her and Zaidu to be on their way. She still finished last. The villagers gobbled their food as if they feared they might never get more. She looked at their thin frames and realized they were no strangers to hunger.

Zaidu rose and stretched, then whistled and walked away without checking that she followed. Shamhat narrowed her eyes. He didn't know any better, but his presumption vexed her anyway. She remained where she was.

He looked vexed himself when he returned for her. "Pay attention, woman."

"You may whistle at your wife as if she were a dog, but I'm a priestess of Inanna."

Zaidu's mouth compressed in apparent exasperation. "Come, then." Again he walked away, but this time looked back after a few steps. "What's wrong now?"

"If you wish me to accompany you, you should say something like 'Lady, would you be so kind as to come with me?'"

Zaidu burst out laughing, and so did several villagers. Heat rose in her face. "This isn't Uruk," Zaidu said. "Come." When she didn't move, he added a grudging "please."

That would have to do for now. She set her bowl down, rose, and followed him.

When they reached the village gate, he said, "Leave your foot coverings here. We'll be in the canal."

She fumed that he had given her another order, but she didn't want her sandals ruined, so she took them off and put them against the palisades. "Why are we going in the canal?"

"To cut reeds."

Reeds again. The villagers had been delighted with the reeds he had built traps with the previous night. Countless times she had recorded gifts and tribute brought to the temple, but never had she wondered where the animal offerings came from. She had assumed people had paddocks and fishponds as the temple did. Instead, they had to work hard to catch and grow their offerings.

When they reached the canal, she stepped gladly into the cool water. The water lifted her skirt, which bobbed on the surface. Even though the dagger Nanna-Ur-Sag had given her was sharp, the reeds were tough. She had blisters on her hands and her hair clung wetly to her face and neck by the time Zaidu signaled they had enough reeds.

She needed to rinse off. She untied and unwound her beaded sash, folded it carefully, and set it on the highest mound of dry land. Then she moved behind the reeds where Zaidu could not see her and dunked herself. She came up shivering and combed her fingers through her hair as the sun dried her and the part of her robe not in the water.

"I don't have a wife," Zaidu said.

She paused, unsure what to say, then continued combing her hair. Zaidu busied himself with something noisy on the other side of the reeds.

"Time to go," Zaidu called. She stepped out of the canal, her skirt clinging to her legs, and went to get her sash.

It wasn't where she had left it.

She scanned the levee, then shaded her eyes and looked downwind, even though it weighed too much to have blown away.

"Are you looking for something?"

"My sash," she said, then gasped. Tied around the middle of a bundle of reeds was her sash. She dashed toward them, and a bead of carnelian fell off and rolled out of sight. Then she noticed the sash's torn edge and her stomach fell. Only half of her sash held these reeds together. The other half bound another bundle .

"You ignorant savage!" If she had had the sash in her hand, she would have strangled him with it. "That sash was a gift from my father, who returned to the clay three months ago. It was worth more than everything in Uzarali put together! Now it's ruined." She swung her arm to slap him.

He grabbed her wrist before her hand connected and looked at her with disdain. "What?" she demanded. His calmness irked her nearly as much as his ruining her sash.

"Out here, a thing has value only if you can eat it or use it. The best use of the sash was to tie reeds together. Now we can carry more."

She yanked her wrist from his grip. "We? That's servant's work." She started toward the village.

"We have no servants."

She stopped and tightened her fists. She hated being out of control, hated not knowing how to behave in this wild place, hated his disrespect and that of the villagers, hated that he was right about the servants. She returned and lifted a bundle of reeds by the sash. The reeds scratched her skin and the beads on the sash sawed into her palm. The bundle's weight grew with every step. When she staggered into the gate of Uzarali, she dropped the reeds with a pleasure as great as if she'd tasted an excellent bread fresh from the oven.

She plunked her bottom onto the bundle, no longer caring about her dignity.

"Get your things." Zaidu tucked his flute into his gazelle skin.

"Now?" Shamhat felt as if she'd put in a full day's work.

"To reach a water hole before dark, we must leave now."

Wearily, Shamhat got up, fetched her basket, and thanked the villagers again for their hospitality. At the gate, Zaidu pointed to two dogs lying against the palisade. Their tails beat joyous rhythms as each chewed something held between its paws.

Her sandals. She reached for one, but jumped back when the dog lunged and growled. Then it ran out of the gate, her sandal still in its mouth. Shamhat groaned and put her forehead against the palisade. Her breath caught in her lungs and she breathed with effort. She would have to walk barefoot across the hot desert sands.

Zaidu, to his credit, waited without complaint.

They needed to reach the water hole before dark. She sighed and stood straight. "I'm ready." Zaidu nodded and they left the village. Soon, they reached the divide between the green lands and the desert. Ahead, as far as she could see, stretched a sea of brown, flat, featureless, endless. A wasteland.

Shamhat walked onto the sand and stopped. She had given up the things that marked her as a priestess of Inanna—her headdress, her necklace of lapis lazuli. She had lost or given up the things that marked her as a noblewoman—her face paints, her cylinder seal, her beaded sash. She had lost even her sandals, something everyone but the poorest of the poor owned. "I am a woman without rank or identity.

"I am no one."

Chapter 10: Attack of the Aurochs

The wilderness
The next day
Zaidu, Shamhat

THEY SPENT THAT DAY SILENT, and the following day as well. The priestess had asked him some questions at first, but he had shushed her each time, telling her she would give them away to predators. In truth, he felt too strange around her to talk—tongue-tied, hot-eared, clumsy, aroused. She stayed silent, even after she started to limp. She was not weak as he had expected for someone so delicate and beautiful. But then, the wise king wouldn't have sent her if she were weak. They moved through the desert as silently as sand on a breeze.

As the sun dropped, the shadows sharpened. Tiny dunes that would have been invisible earlier now cast crisp black shadows. It was the most dangerous time of day: The world became dark and light, with no in-betweens, and nothing looked as it should. Far away, he saw the long shadows of trees surrounding tonight's destination, a small water hole.

To the south, a dust cloud rose and approached as he watched. He scanned the horizon and saw no other; he licked his finger and lifted it to the wind. The wind came from a different direction. The cloud was not a sandstorm, which could be deadly. Still, anything unknown was a potential danger.

He took the bow from his shoulder. "We need to reach the water hole quickly." He quickened his pace, and the priestess hobbled faster. Alone, he could reach the water hole and climb a tree easily.

But with Shamhat slowing him down, he feared the cloud—and whatever it contained—would reach them where they had no cover.

He kept his gaze moving, from the water hole to the dust cloud, then sweeping the horizon. Large shapes moved within the dust. A herd of animals, he assumed. Sweat rolled down his forehead, and Shamhat panted.

"Stop. We'll wait here." He threw himself down, pulled an arrow from his quiver, and nocked it. Shamhat stumbled a few steps forward and fell flat.

"Won't we be seen here in the open?" she whispered.

He glanced at her white covering and black hair, both contrasts with the brown of the sand. "Animals often don't notice things that don't move."

"I'll be still." She did as she said, but murmured under her breath, "Inanna, Queen of Heaven, protect us. Protect your daughter Shamhat and the trapper Zaidu from evil. Protect your daughter Shamhat and the trapper Zaidu from the men of the desert. Protect your daughter Shamhat and the trapper Zaidu from the animals of the desert. Inanna of many sixties of *me*, keep us safe from harm, keep us from sinning."

The cloud shifted and headed straight toward them. The smell preceded it, the hot, musky smell of grazing animals and the rotten-egg stink of their farts. He could now see a huge black animal and several large reddish ones. Zaidu sucked in his breath as the creatures snorted. Aurochs had mean tempers at the best of times. He did not wish to find out their mood during a stampede.

"We have to run," he whispered. She shifted her weight to her knees and hands.

"Now!" He burst up, bow in hand. Shamhat ran for a few steps, then tripped on her garment. She fell, grabbing her ankle. The aurochs would be on them in moments. Shamhat crawled away, looking at him over her shoulder with eyes wide with fear.

Zaidu drew and shot, drew and shot, drew and shot, aiming at the king of the group, the black bull. The soft sand shook under the giant beasts' hooves. The king aurochs still ran, arrows piercing his tough hide, his shoulder well above Zaidu's head, his vicious horns wider than Zaidu was tall and pointed right at him.

He drew and shot, drew and shot, drew and shot.

The black aurochs stumbled, bellowing. The noise seemed to startle the cows. They swerved, scattering. The king aurochs pawed the ground and fell. Zaidu took one deep breath before a cow lowered her sharp horns and ran at Shamhat.

He had time for only one shot. It would have to be a good, clean shot, or Shamhat would die. Zaidu shouted to get the cow's attention. It lifted its heavy head and swung it toward him. He let his arrow fly.

Shamhat had sense enough to scramble out of the way. The cow fell, the arrow piercing its eye. The other cows ran on, leaving their king behind. Bellowing, the bull struggled to stand, blood running from its many wounds and its beady gaze on Zaidu. Zaidu snatched his last arrow and fell forward to his knees, aiming at the bull aurochs' underbelly. The bull swung its head. The weight of the huge, lethal horns slowed their turn. Zaidu flattened, and the horns passed over him. Then he rose to his knees and shot. Despite his awkward position, the arrow flew true and pierced the bull. Moaning, thrashing, the bull roused a choking cloud of sand.

Coughing, Zaidu backed away, keeping his gaze on the downed aurochs. The exhilaration and joy of combat fled. He sensed something behind him and whirled, whipping his knife up. Instead of a maddened cow, he found Shamhat. She stood on her uninjured leg, eyes wide as she stared at his knife a few fingers from her belly.

"I—" She took several shaky breaths. "I thought you might need my knife." She held out a bronze dagger.

"We're safe for now. Can you walk?"

She shook her head as she put her dagger in its sheath and then into her basket. "I can only hop."

Zaidu glanced at the setting sun. They would not make it to the water hole before night fell black on the desert.

Shamhat's stomach twisted with nervousness as Zaidu glanced between her injured ankle, the aurochs, and the water hole far in the distance. She could not hop that far on her blistered foot.

She had a flash of memory. When she was small, a lame beggar regularly sat outside the gates of the Eanna with his begging bowl. The man used a reed to help him walk.

"Zaidu, could you go the water hole and bring me a reed? A stout one that can support my weight as I walk?"

"No time." Zaidu slung her over his shoulder as easily as if she had been a cat. Then he ran.

The arms around her legs were corded with muscle, and she nestled nicely against his neck on his broad shoulders. She felt safe and secure. Like a bird she flew, her hair streaming. She closed her gritty eyes against the dust and breathed in the refreshing cool breeze that distracted her from the crusts in her nostrils and the pain of her blisters and injured ankle. She felt no anger at the trapper for touching her, only gratitude, as if the city and temple rules that had always guided her behavior did not apply in the wilderness.

Soon, the air had a scent again. Except for the wild cows, she had smelled nothing except her and Zaidu's sweat since they entered the desert. But now, she smelled vegetation and damp earth. Zaidu slowed to a walk, and leaves brushed her legs. Zaidu set her down with her back against something hard, and she opened her eyes. She blinked away the blur. Barely enough light remained for her to see they had reached the water hole and were surrounded by grasses and trees.

Shamhat stretched her sore muscles. "Is this what every day is like for you?" she croaked.

He laughed without humor and moved to the water hole. He refilled his water skin, drank his fill, then handed it to her. "Aurochs are stupid and always angry. We're lucky to be alive."

Her hand shook so hard more water spilled on her chin than landed in her mouth. Because Zaidu had acted calmly, she had not realized the attack was deadly. "I prayed, and the Goddess protected us. She's here in the desert with us."

"I didn't see any Goddess, only my own two arms shooting arrows."

Shamhat gave him back the water skin. "Inanna guided your aim."

"Why didn't She guide the aurochs on a different path?"

A cold shiver ran down Shamhat's back. He would incite the Goddess's wrath with his disrespect. "Praise Inanna!" she exclaimed. "Greatest of the Gods, forgive our sins and protect us!" Then she spoke in whisper. "Shh. Inanna can be vengeful. She banished Her husband Dumuzi to the Netherworld, where the dark Goddess Ereshkigal reigns, because he usurped Inanna's throne." Shamhat took two loaves of barley bread from her basket and passed him one. "When you speak of Her, be humble and respectful. And add a good dose of flattery."

"I don't know your Gods and don't worship Them. Why haven't They struck me down?"

Shamhat yawned, too tired to think. She pulled a cloak from her basket and wrapped it around her. In all her years of training at the temple, never had the role of the nomads been discussed. All people had been created to serve the Gods. But how did people like Zaidu, who had no temple to work for or give offerings to, fit into the Gods' plan for the world?

She would have to figure it out before she had to teach the wild man about civilization.

Chapter 11: Debate

The wilderness
The next day
Zaidu

S MOKE DRIFTED ABOVE THE WATER HOLE. Zaidu dropped his
burden of aurochs horn and aurochs hide and ran toward the smoke,
stopping at the outer edge of vegetation. His empty stomach
rumbled at the smell of fish. Cooked fish, not raw as they had eaten the
previous night in the dark. He circled the water hole until he could see the
fire. He let out a sigh of relief when he saw Shamhat. She held several thin
reeds, each skewering a small fish, over the fire as she sang softly.

The priestess was not the woman he had expected her to be. She
had not complained once on the trip, even though she had given up
her city things, burned her feet, and twisted her ankle. He had
assumed city people were weak and useless. But Shamhat would make
a suitable wife for a trapper.

He retrieved his trophies. The aurochs skin, with its many
arrow holes, might not fetch a good price, but the horn would.

Shamhat whirled when he came toward the water hole, the huge
horn making as much noise as six people when he carried it through
the trees. She relaxed when she saw it was Zaidu. "I thought you
might have abandoned me."

"I went back to the kill."

Her gaze flicked from his prizes to the small fish roasting over
the fire. "No meat?"

"If I could have carried more, I'd have taken the other horn. We
can eat dates for another day." He knelt by the edge of the spring and

rubbed himself with water to get rid of the sticky blood. Skinning the aurochs had speckled him with gore.

"The horn?" Her brow rose. "Why do *you* need a statue or drinking horn?"

He grinned. "No one needs a statue or drinking horn. But a trader will give me grain or blocks of salt for it and take it to the city to sell to those who *think* they need one."

He found it easier to talk to her now. He still thought her beautiful, especially her eyes, but without face paint and ornaments, she seemed less Godlike. She offered him a skewered fish and some dried dates, and they ate in silence.

Afterward, he sliced the end of a stout reed and pulled it apart so Shamhat could put her armpit in it. He shouldered his prizes, his muscles straining under the horn, which was longer than an arm, and they set off. Tonight, they would reach his and *Ada*'s tent.

The weight slowed him, and even leaning on the reed, Shamhat kept pace. After a while, she said, "You asked me a question yesterday. Do you remember?"

"I asked whether you could walk on your injured ankle."

She tossed her head like an impatient antelope. "No, later. You said you didn't worship the Gods and asked why the Gods had not struck you down. I think I know the answer."

The answer wasn't important for survival, so it wasn't important at all. He replied with a grunt.

"The Gods created people to serve Them, yet you apparently don't."

Her comment irritated him like a skin worn inside out. "Yet here I am."

"It's because of trade." Her voice quickened, and against his will, he paid more attention. "The skins and meat and other goods you trade end up in the city. Some go to Inanna and An directly, and others to the workers who grow Their food."

"So I exist to serve the city."

Her eyebrows arched like drawn bows. "Of course." She made a sweeping gesture that took in the land around them. "There's nothing here. People were created from clay to serve the Gods in Their cities."

"And yet here I am," he repeated, his tone revealing his irritation.

She appeared not to notice. "After I tame the wild man, you should come to the city with us." She glanced at his chest and shoulder muscles, which bulged under the weight of his load, then looked away. "Once you've been to the barber and the baths and gotten a proper fleece to wear, you'd quickly find a job."

His laugh carried across the desert. "How do you spend your days?"

"I feed the Goddess four times a day. We sing, present Her with beer and food, and bring in the new statuettes that petitioners have left. Sometimes my brother summons me for family business. The rest of the time I do as the *en*-priest instructs. Mostly, I keep records and accounts—how many *gur*-cubes of barley come in and where they are distributed, and the same for wheat, jars of beer, sheep, cows. When I have free time, I compose hymns to the Goddess."

"You spend your life doing what others want—your Goddess, the *en*-priest, the king, your brother. I'm free, but you live like a penned sheep."

"I'm a priestess in the world's greatest city." She swatted away insects with more vigor than needed. "You live barely better than an animal." Her voice got louder and more scornful. "You don't wear real clothes or jewelry; you have no king or council; you can't read or write. You don't even wear a cylinder seal."

Zaidu was having too much fun goading her to stop. "You. Count. Sheep."

She put her hands on her hips and tossed her hair. "It's an important job. I make sure the Goddess receives all the tribute that She is owed and that those who depend on Her receive their share."

"I do what I want, when I want. I rely on no one."

"Like the aurochs of yesterday."

He puffed out his chest as much as he could under his heavy burden. "I'm no aurochs, running about in a useless rage. I choose what I do. No temple takes what I make and gives it to others. I am better off than anyone in Uruk, even King Gilgamesh."

She gave him a look of disbelief. "How can that be?"

"He's not a happy man. I am."

She hopped as she twisted toward him. "Not happy? He has everything he wants."

"He's lonely. He believes the wild man is a friend foretold in a dream." Zaidu recounted the dream the king had told him.

Shamhat sucked in her breath. "*Meliea*! A friend?"

Zaidu narrowed his eyes. "Why would that be so bad?"

"Nanna-Ur-Sag dreamed of the wild man, too. He believed the wild man can bring Gilgamesh to heel."

"You want to undermine your own leader? Is that how 'civilized' people behave?"

"Not undermine him. Merely humble him so he can be the king he's meant to be and so the Gods don't punish Uruk for his sins."

Zaidu kicked the sand and cursed. "I wanted only a small thing, to stop the wild man from looting my traps. Now I'm caught between the two most powerful men in Uruk."

"So am I. The king holds my son hostage."

He staggered. "Your son!" The *en*-priest and the king's servant had both ordered him not to couple with Shamhat because she belonged to Inanna. All this time he had burned for her but left her alone. Yet she had a son. How? When? "The king took your son? I don't understand."

"Inanna-Ama-Mu's a hostage. To ensure I obey the king's orders." Shamhat caught up to him, her breathing ragged. "I'll admit the wilderness does have one advantage over the city. No politics."

"*Alala*!" *Ada* exclaimed, running his hands along the aurochs horn Zaidu had placed across his lap. "The traders will pay much for this. And is that a hide I smell?"

"I skinned the aurochs." He gave his father the hide. *Ada* stroked it from side to side, sticking a different finger in each arrow hole.

He held up eight fingers. "There are as many holes as fingers I hold up."

"Eight holes," Shamhat interjected.

"Your wife talks too much," *Ada* said. "I think a trader will give me a good price for the skin despite the holes. It's large and has few scars."

Zaidu rolled his neck and shoulders. The trip had been long, and sitting by a fire was bliss. "Tomorrow, perhaps we'll have more luck, when I take Shamhat to meet the wild man." He picked up his hammerstone and some flint. He needed to replace the arrowheads he had lost.

"What? So eager to be rid of her already? Don't waste her on the wild man. Trade her to the shepherds for a ewe."

Zaidu grinned at Shamhat, and she rolled her eyes. Zaidu had explained the king had sent Shamhat to tame the wild man, but *Ada* couldn't or wouldn't believe him.

The next morning when Zaidu awoke, Shamhat was already up. She had stoked the fire and now knelt nearby, shells and small dishes in front of her. She pulled a notched piece of ivory through her hair. Zaidu propped himself on an elbow. Her hair fell into smooth black waves that gleamed in the firelight. Murmuring a prayer to Inanna, she took a tiny ivory stick, dipped it in a dish, and drew dark lines across her upper and lower eyelids while looking at a polished disc of copper. She repeated the process with another stick and dish. She added a few drops of water from her waterskin to a shell and mixed the contents with yet another small ivory stick, this one with a round, scooped bowl at the end, and then rubbed some on her cheeks and lips.

The ritual must be part of her magic. He had been struck with awe the first time he had seen her, and now as he watched her, he felt not only awe but also warmth. Saying another prayer, she scraped wax from the end of a tube of polished alabaster, placed her finger over the now-bare end, and shook the stone. An unusual smell, like sesame oil, juniper, and honey all at once, wafted toward him. She stroked her finger down either side of her neck, leaving a shiny trail.

She replaced the wax on the stone and put lids on the dishes and shell. She looked up and caught his eye, and a slow smile grew. "If the wild man looks at me like that, I should have no trouble taming him." Her voice was a low flute, sweet and alluring.

He crawled toward her, and she stopped him with an upheld hand.

"You have a son," he said. "You did it with someone." He awkwardly stroked her cheek and felt the blood pulse in her neck. "Why not me?"

She shivered, then pushed his hand away. "I acted at the temple's command. Part of the New Year's festival. Otherwise, I'm bound by a vow of chastity."

Zaidu came back to himself. "Vow of chastity. Right." He rubbed his face with his hand. "Then why—" He gestured at her face.

"How did you think I would tame the wild man?"

Her words punched him in the gut, and he hated the wild man more than he had ever hated anything. "You're a priestess. I thought you'd use magic. Prayer. Rituals. Offerings."

"I don't use magic, only the *me* of Inanna." Shamhat must have guessed his confusion because she added, "the *me* are divine powers— music, art, leatherworking, kingship, everything that makes a city. To tame the wild man, I'll use the *me* of sexual intercourse."

Zaidu clenched his fists and glanced toward his bow. He imagined an arrow piercing the chest of the wild man, and the wild man falling to the ground dead. The image pleased him.

Chapter 12: Awakening

The water hole
The next three days
Shamhat, the wild man, Shamhat, Zaidu

THE FIRST DAY SHAMHAT SPENT AT THE WATER HOLE with the trapper, the wild man did not come. Zaidu had kept busy building new traps. After the twelfth time Shamhat checked her reflection in the murky water and after countless adjustments of her shawl, she had asked whether she could help, and he showed her how to hold the reeds so he could tie them together more quickly. They worked silently, ever alert for the sound of gazelles.

The second day they spent at the water hole, the wild man did not come. Zaidu had persuaded Shamhat not to wear any perfume because it might scare the animals, and she had colored only her eyes. Quietly, as he wove a basket from reeds, Zaidu told her the names of each bird and beast that came to the water hole, how to identify them by sound and scent, and the best way to capture them. She in turn, just as quietly, taught him to count.

The third day they spent at the water hole, she feared the wild man would not come. She left her face unpainted because Zaidu thought the colors might scare the wild man. She no longer felt the need for them to talk, and she barely thought of the wild man. She had learned to be patient and to appreciate quiet. Not that the water hole was truly silent, once Zaidu had taught her to listen. Insects whizzed by, birds called to each other, and lizards scurried through the bushes.

"If I were home today, I'd be dressed in my best for New Year's." Shamhat closed her eyes, picturing the excited crowds clogging the streets and the boats on the canals. "The king and Inanna will leave the city from the—"

Zaidu put up his hand. Leaves rustled as Zaidu half-rose. "I hear gazelles." He shimmied up a palm tree as easily as she would climb a ladder. He looked around, then slid down.

"What did you see?" Shamhat asked, her throat tight. Nervousness hit her like her father's hand, hard and unexpected.

"It's the wild man's herd. He's leading them here." Zaidu picked up his bow and took an arrow from his quiver.

Shamhat stood and put her hand on the bow. "No. I must take him to the king."

Zaidu glared at her with fierceness and anger. "I won't let him hurt you," he growled.

She could tell he meant he wouldn't let the wild man have her. "I must do what I came for, what you brought me here to do." She stood, took a deep breath, and then walked toward the sound of gazelles, her hips swaying and her eyes partially closed. *I am the earthly representation of Inanna, Queen of Heaven. All men are mine if I desire.*

She walked until vegetation gave way to desert. The wild man stopped, but the thirsty gazelles parted like a river around an island and flowed past her. The wild man stepped from one foot to another and fingered something beneath his beard. He cocked his head and took a step backward. He was about to bolt.

Shamhat sang a lullaby, one her mother had sung to her, as she slowly unwrapped her shawl. The wild man scratched his head, his face scrunched in puzzlement. She took off her robe. He took a few steps toward her. Shamhat lay down on the sand, her arms beckoning.

The wild man's eyes darkened with lust, and he started toward her, desire outweighing fear. Then his gaze flicked, and his face reddened with anger.

Shamhat checked behind her. Zaidu stood there, raising his bow. The wild man bellowed and ran at Zaidu.

* * *

Enemy. The man who dug pits to trap gazelles and antelopes. The man who made traps for small animals that do no harm. The man who killed his gazelle sister and still wore her skin.

He would frighten him. The enemy would run. This time, he would chase. The enemy would stay away.

The smooth and rounded man stood. He had forgotten this man. He slowed. The smooth man shoved the enemy. The enemy backed away. He growled at the enemy and looked at the smooth man.

This one smelled different. Not of death but life. No fear, no anger. Openness. Trust. He reached out and touched. Soft. His body reacted to the smooth one in a way it never had to any animal or man.

He tried to remember his childhood. There were several kinds of men. Boys. Girls. Men. And women. Women who sang songs like this one.

This one was a woman, a lifebearer, a milkgiver. Like his sister gazelles.

He looked down at himself. Each year, in the season when the weather got cooler, his brother gazelles played games with the sister gazelles, marching after them and prancing. The games ended with the male gazelles mounting the females. He had thought it a silly game until now.

The woman put her hand on his abdomen and ran it up through his fur.

No, not fur. People had . . . hair.

He didn't bother marching or prancing.

He grabbed her by the long tail of hair that hung down her back. She wrapped her arms around him. He fell on her.

Shamhat knew everything rode on this moment—the king's assignment, her son's safety, her brother's life, the future of Uruk. It wasn't enough the wild man wanted her now. He needed to want her long enough to accompany her to the city.

The wild man knew what he wanted to do, but not quite how to do it, other than gazelle-style. Shamhat used her temple training to teach him the arts of Inanna.

He was an enthusiastic student.

She remained half-aware of Zaidu nearby. He didn't interrupt, but he didn't go away, either. He paced the rushes back and forth, back and forth, startling jerboas and lizards from the bushes. She shared his frustration. Traveling through the desert, she and Zaidu had gotten to know each other in a way she had known few other men.

She pretended the wild man's grunts were Zaidu's grunts, that his tongue was Zaidu's tongue. She couldn't maintain the fantasy. The wild man's size, furriness, and musky smell made him seem more bear than man.

She lost all sense of time. Gradually, the wild man began to mix words with his grunts. At last he rolled over, sated. She stroked his face, murmuring sweet words. He touched her cheek and struggled to shape his lips to form a word. She held her breath.

"Wo-man."

"Yes!" So the wild man hadn't always been wild. That would make civilizing him easier. "My name is Shamhat. What is your name?"

He scrunched his eyes, then shook his head with frustration. He leapt up and, without looking back, loped to the water hole and his gazelle family.

The gazelles lifted their heads, their nostrils widening as they sniffed. A young male took a few stiff but quick steps and leaped high in the air, a signal of danger, Zaidu had told her. Then the gazelle streaked into the desert. As one, the others turned and followed.

The wild man pelted after them. He caught up, but the young male leaped high in the air again. The gazelles ran faster, leaving the wild man behind.

He stood, shoulders slumped, staring into the distance with his hands curled like a baby's. When Shamhat could no longer see the gazelles, the wild man sat on the ground and wailed, the cry of a man who'd lost everything.

His howl of despair tore something in her chest. Ashamed, Shamhat bowed her head. Tears rolled down her face. She had taken this man's innocence without any concern for his well-being. "Inanna, great Mother, please protect the wild man. Inanna, guardian of the *me*, let him share in the gifts of civilization and be glad of this day."

She picked up her cloak, walked out to the wild man, and wrapped it around him. He plucked at it with one hand, but she put her own hand over his. "Come. I will care for you."

He looked up, his eyes glazed with tears, and stood. Shamhat took him by the hand and led him toward the water hole. "My name is Shamhat," she told him again, pointing to herself. "What is your name?"

His face crinkled as he thought. "*Dumu.*"

Dumu. Child. He remembered only what he had been called as a boy. "The God Enki designed humans," she told him. "Your new name will remind you that you are human, not animal. From now on, your name is 'Enki's Creation.' Enki-Du."

Zaidu swatted at every insect that bit him and kicked through the grasses around the water hole. His guts cramped as if he had eaten bad meat. He hadn't watched Shamhat with the wild man, but he had heard the two of them rutting. Shamhat had been a willing sacrifice for her Goddess. In-between the wild man's bellows had sounded a woman's sighs and moans of pleasure.

Afterward, when the gazelles rejected the wild man, he should have been overjoyed. He had gone to King Gilgamesh with a problem, and the king had solved it.

Instead, he felt urges and emotions he didn't have names for. He wanted to challenge the wild man to a fight. He wanted to drag Shamhat from the wild man. He wanted to couple with Shamhat himself so his seed could displace the wild man's.

His father had taught him early, through example and many cuffs to the ear, to restrain his behavior, to think before acting, to do nothing to incite a wild beast. So he ignored the urges and walked with a relaxed, slow pace toward the wild man and Shamhat.

The wild man shoved Shamhat behind him so violently she fell down. Then he bared his teeth and growled as he threw himself at Zaidu.

"Enkidu, no! Friend! Friend!" Shamhat scrambled to her feet and grabbed the wild man's—Enkidu's—arm.

His heart shushing in his ears like water lapping at a bank, Zaidu had his knife out and at the giant's throat before he realized the man had listened to Shamhat. Enkidu pulled his lips back, showing yellowed teeth, but didn't resume his attack. Shamhat linked her hand with Enkidu's, and Zaidu could not tear his gaze away.

"What do we do with him now?" Zaidu asked Shamhat.

"I'll take him to the shepherds. They can help me teach Enkidu what he needs to know."

Zaidu had the water hole back. He could trap again, and he and his father would eat well. Everything would be normal and right, as it had been before the wild man had started coming to the water hole, as he had wanted.

"Why the shepherds? Why not me?" he blurted.

Shamhat colored.

"You keep saying how much better city life is. I'll go with you to hear Enkidu's lessons. I'll decide for myself which is better, your life or mine."

"City life," Shamhat answered immediately. Then she smiled, and nothing else existed. "Come to the shepherds' camp anyway. You might be useful."

Chapter 13: Bread, Beer, and Baths

The wilderness
The next morning
Shamhat, Zaidu

THE STINK OF BURNING SHEEP DUNG and the aroma of cooking flat bread woke Shamhat the next morning, and she wriggled free of Enkidu's embrace. She had succeeded at her first step, separating Enkidu from the animals. It was time to train Enkidu to be human again. He still wore her shawl, its embroidered rosettes at odds with his brawny frame. He was so large the shawl was a short skirt on him. The sight energized her. He was more muscular than Gilgamesh and almost as tall. He could be the city's savior.

She shook Enkidu's shoulder. "It's time to learn to eat and drink like a civilized man."

He yawned and stretched, knocking over a tent pole. The tent fell on him, and he beat at it with his fists, shouting.

Shamhat lifted the skin and held out her hand as if to a child. "Come, Enkidu." She led him outside, where Zaidu's gaze on her made her skin prickle. She ignored him.

Several breads stood stacked near the fire where Adapa's wife cooked. "May we?" she asked Adapa. He gave her a bread. She pulled on Enkidu's shoulders to get him to crouch.

She held the flatbread out to him. He narrowed his eyes with suspicion. "Take it," she urged. "This is bread, what humans eat."

He put out one finger to touch it, then jerked it back. "Hot."

"Taste it. It's good."

Enkidu took the bread from her and licked the top. His eyes widened, and his mouth dropped open. He took another lick and then a bite. A smile spread across his face as he chewed. He stuffed the rest of his bread into his mouth and grabbed another.

"Zaidu, please see whether the shepherds can spare some beer," Shamhat said. Zaidu answered with a glare, and Adapa's wife got up and went into one of the tents. Enkidu gobbled down more bread.

"*Ashe!*" Adapa cried to the other shepherds. "Our guest eats like a wild boar!" Adapa's wife returned with a *kuli*. Adapa turned to Shamhat. "Can he drink as much as he eats?"

"Let's see." Shamhat took the ceramic beerpot from Adapa's wife and sniffed it. *Ebla*. She didn't like the watery beer herself, but it would be good for Enkidu's first taste.

Enkidu wiped his mouth with his arm and relaxed backward. "Bread good."

"Enkidu, this is beer, what humans drink." She handed him the heavy *kuli*. Again, he stared at it, uncertain what to do. Shamhat stuck her finger in the *ebla* and wiped it on Enkidu's lips. His nose wrinkled at the smell. "Taste it," she urged. He licked his lips. Again his eyes lit up, and he stuck his huge hand into the *kuli* and then slurped beer off it.

The shepherds laughed and slapped their legs, and Zaidu's frown softened. "No, Enkidu, like this." Shamhat grasped the *kuli* around its wide middle, lifted it to her lips, and sipped. "See? It's easy."

"Now I drink." Enkidu took the *kuli* and chugged all the *ebla* down in the amount of time it took Shamhat to count to twelve. He threw the *kuli* aside. "More!"

Adapa's wife ran back to the tent and brought out more beer. "I'll wager ten soft cheeses against a pair of gazelle horns that he can't drink more than three *kuli*s of beer," Adapa said to Zaidu, handing Enkidu another beerpot full of *ebla*.

"Done!" Zaidu said. "Go, Enkidu!" Other shepherds shouted their own encouragements as Adapa glowered. Enkidu finished the second *kuli* as easily as he had the first. Zaidu kept handing him *kuli*s, and Enkidu kept drinking until he had emptied seven.

Shamhat could not keep from giggling. Enkidu's face, what she could see of it, shone bright red. His eyes crinkled with happiness as they looked in different directions. "*Alala!*" he cried. He leapt up and waved his arms.

"Dance, Enkidu!" the shepherds shouted. They put their arms around each other's shoulders and skipped about. Enkidu mimicked them for a few steps, then stumbled drunkenly and fell. He roared with laughter when he hit the ground.

"I like human!"

"You're not quite there yet, Enkidu." Shamhat thought he was drunk enough for the next step. "Zaidu, shepherds, could you please hold him still and upright?"

Enkidu's howls of laughter changed to howls of fear when Shamhat pulled out her knife.

Zaidu sweated and grunted as he and the shepherds struggled to hold the giant still. Twice Enkidu broke free, and twice Shamhat's gentle voice and soft words persuaded him to sit again.

Shamhat stroked Enkidu's head as if he were her child. "All these men have gotten haircuts and survived. You will too."

The beer seemed to overtake Enkidu at last, and Zaidu's rival slumped against him, half asleep. "Now, Shamhat," Zaidu urged.

She started with the hair that hung below his waist. She grabbed a hank at shoulder-blade level and sawed off the hair above. Five more rounds, and she was done. Zaidu coiled the arm-long pieces of hair and set them aside for netmaking.

"Now the beard." Shamhat grimaced as she surveyed the tangled nest that hung nearly to Enkidu's waist. She cut the beard off straight across at the top of his chest, a style Zaidu had seen many men in Uruk wearing.

Something dangled from a dirty, twisted strip of leather, something long and curved and creamy like ivory.

Zaidu hefted it in his hand, and his spine tingled. "*Ashe!* A lion's tooth."

Shamhat's eyes widened. "How'd he get that?"

"He killed a lion. That's his trophy," Adapa answered.

"Without weapons? Great Inanna, protect us from his strength." Shamhat stared at the tooth, then squared her shoulders and announced, "Next, a bath."

Zaidu felt a rush of alarm. "How?"

"We'll take him to the water hole."

Zaidu harrumphed. "By 'we' do you mean the men?"

Shamhat gave him an arrogant stare, one Zaidu had become well familiar with. "Of course. That's not a job for a priestess, even if I could carry such a load. Hurry, before he sobers up."

Zaidu and the shepherds looked at each other and by common, unspoken accord, they hauled Enkidu upright, and the largest shepherd threw Enkidu's arm around his neck. One shepherd stayed behind to guard the sheep. Zaidu and the others supported Enkidu from the back and other side. Together, they lurched toward the water hole, Shamhat following behind with a vial of oil.

All the men needed baths by the time they had dragged Enkidu to the water hole under the hot sun. After getting Enkidu into a shallow, shaded part of the spring and making him sit, Zaidu took off his skin and jumped in. He dunked his head, allowing the warm water to steal the heat from his face and scalp. When he could no longer hold his breath, he popped up, letting the water run in cooling streams down his body as he twisted his beard and hair in turn to squeeze out the water.

He did not want to look at Shamhat. He wanted to focus on the pleasant feeling of not being hot. But he stole a glance over anyway. A knot formed in his chest. Shamhat sat in the water, Enkidu in front of her, leaning against her. The bath was done. Shamhat worked her fingers through Enkidu's hair, unknotting it so it flowed like the dark current of a rainy-season stream.

Shamhat spoke gently, but too softly for him to hear the words, and laughed like a carefree child. Enkidu laughed too, a rough "haw-haw" that startled Adapa so much he fell backwards into the water. Zaidu knotted his fists. If only *he* were the one relaxed in Shamhat's arms, his naked back pressed against breasts covered only by thin, wet linen, her arms brushing against him as she ran her fingers through his hair and rubbed him with oil.

"I'm going back to camp," he told the shepherds.

"*Ashe!*" Adapa scooped up a handful of water and threw it at him. "How will we get the wild man back?"

"When he's sober, he can walk on his own." Or if Zaidu was lucky, he might drown. He put on his skin and broke into a lope. Although he had not had a woman in a long time, he had respected Shamhat's vow of chastity. The people of the desert had a strong code of honor, and he had recognized her vow as something similar.

Now she broke that vow. Perhaps he could have borne it if she had made her sacrifice with fear and tears and prayer. But she had enjoyed it. The memory of her moans and sighs forced his feet to run faster. He felt tricked, betrayed, disgusted.

And yet he still wanted her. He would find a way to have her.

Night had fallen on the camp, a grayish night lit by the banked fires, the nearly full Moon, and uncountable sixties of stars. Zaidu huddled by a fire, sipping a *kuli* of beer and watching Shamhat's tent.

She lay alone, probably asleep, and he should sleep too. But he kept watch anyway, dreading and expecting Enkidu to lumber up and go in to join her. The Moon traveled across the bowl of heaven on its preordained journey, and still Enkidu had not come.

Shamhat came out of her tent, a blanket wrapped around her. She looked about, and her gaze fixed on Zaidu. She padded toward him and sat down next to him and the fire.

The fire's heat seemed to increase. "Beer?" he asked, offering her the *kuli*. She nodded, took a few sips, and handed it back. He fished about for something to say, but she spoke first.

"Have you seen Enkidu?"

Zaidu slumped, and a breath escaped. "No." She had not come out to visit him.

"I haven't seen him since we returned from the water hole. He went off with some shepherds. I'm worried."

"It may take more than bread, beer, and a bath to make him fully human."

"His face—he doesn't look like the black-headed people or like your people. Have you noticed?"

"No." When Shamhat was around, she was all he noticed.

"His lips and nose are too large for his face. His lower jaw sticks out, and his hands and feet are huge."

"He must come from far away."

"But he speaks our language." She shifted. "Why's it taking him so long to come back?"

"Maybe he found the gazelles."

"No!" Shamhat ran her hand through her hair. The mussed waves spilled over her shoulders. "If he did, I'll find him again. I have to."

"Not if you don't go back to the city."

She lifted her head and looked at him. Not just at him, but into his eyes, as if she saw beyond what the Gods had made from clay and into his *zi*, his soul. "Have you ever known another woman as well as me?"

He started at the intimate question. Every so often, traders brought women who could be bought for a night or for life. But he rarely learned their names, much less anything else.

"Other than my brother, I have never known a man as well as I know you. Yet I know you little."

"Too little?" He held his breath for the answer.

"Enough to wonder what my life would have been like if I hadn't been chosen as a child to serve Inanna." She stood and wrapped her blanket about her more tightly. "I'm going to look for Enkidu."

Something slithered in the sand nearby. "I'll go with you." Zaidu set down his *kuli,* dipped the end of a reed in the fire to use as a torch, and stood. "I know the sounds of animals that hunt at night."

She waited for him to lead the way. He headed toward the sheepfold because Enkidu had gone off with the shepherds. They walked in silence, as usual, but it was a comforting silence.

"Good health to you!" Adapa's voice called. Zaidu held his torch further forward, revealing the outlines of Adapa and his nephew, Hanzamu.

"Have you seen Enkidu?" Shamhat held out her hands imploringly. "He's been gone for a long time."

"He asked us if he could meet the sheep." Adapa stretched and yawned. "We took him to the sheepfold, and he's been there since."

"That's why we're coming back to camp," Hanzamu added. "Enkidu said he would guard the sheep at night." Adapa clapped his hand on his nephew's shoulder, and they walked on.

"I'm going to check on him," Shamhat said.

She didn't protest when Zaidu went with her. At the sheepfold, they saw Enkidu's huge form silhouetted in the moonlight. He moved among the sheep, touching their faces as if to learn each individually. A lamb bleated, and Enkidu picked it up and held it close, stroking it. When a ewe baaed, Enkidu carried the lamb to it, squatted, and placed the lamb under the ewe and guided its mouth to a teat.

Zaidu had reasons to hate the wild man. But his guts tingled in pity and sadness for him. No matter what Shamhat did, Enkidu would always belong among the animals.

A huge shadow flew over the wall into the sheepfold with an ear-blasting roar, and Shamhat screamed. Zaidu stepped in front of her and grabbed for his bow.

Chapter 14: Danger In the Sheepfold

The wilderness
That night
Enkidu, Shamhat

A CREATURE PADDED ACROSS THE SAND. A lion. It would eat his new family as it had his first one. Enkidu's liver filled with rage. He jumped up from where he had squatted next to the lamb, and a roaring lioness flew over the wall of the sheepfold, clamped its jaws around the neck of a ewe, and flipped it to the ground. The other sheep ran. But the pen kept them from escaping.

Enkidu bellowed and jumped high like a stotting male gazelle. The lioness lifted its eyes from where it half-lay on the sheep to look at him. It growled deep in its throat, but did not loosen its hold. Outside, the humans screamed and yelled, their words without meaning.

Enkidu fingered the tooth on his chest and bounded toward the lioness. It snarled and stood, dropping the sheep. The ewe lay limp and bloody on the ground. Its mouth moved but no sound came out. He jumped onto the lioness's back.

Reason deserted him. One goal dominated him, body and mind: Kill. The lioness roared and twisted to throw Enkidu off. But he dug his hands into its scruff.

The lioness snapped at him, then dropped and rolled onto its back. Enkidu jumped free. The lioness landed on dirt instead of him. It rolled up and stared at him, its head low, its front legs wide apart, its shoulders raised. Then its tail twitched, and it coughed. It stalked toward him, the muscles in its shoulders rippling.

Enkidu walked backwards until he bumped into a wall of the sheepfold. He turned and kicked. The mud bricks broke apart and fell outside. Now his new family could escape.

He edged away from the escape hole. The lioness turned to keep him in view. It growled and crouched.

He jumped at the same time it did. His feet and its nose met with a thud. The lioness blinked and grunted as they fell and landed in a sprawl. He regained his feet first. He pulled off the cloth Shamhat had told him to wear and jumped onto the back of the lioness's head, pinning it to the ground. He might not have teeth or claws, but he matched it in size. It kicked with its hind legs, struggling to rise. He wadded up Shamhat's garment and waited.

The lioness opened its mouth in a growl. Enkidu yanked back the upper jaw and stuffed the garment in the lioness's throat.

The lioness thrashed and batted at its nose and mouth. It paid no attention to Enkidu. He wrapped both of his arms about its head and twisted until he heard the snap.

Something that sounded like an insect whizzed by as he dropped the head. A reed quivered in the lioness's side. He spun. Man-Who-Wears-Sister's-Skin stood with his weapon. Enkidu drew back his upper lip and growled. This was *his* kill.

He pulled the reed from the lioness's side. Tied onto the end was a sharp-edged stone. He removed it, pulled back the lioness's upper lip, and began cutting out a trophy tooth.

Shamhat shivered. Despite the blanket wrapped around her, she was so cold her fingers were stiff and she could barely move them. She stared at Enkidu, his muscles glowing with sweat in the moonlight, his chest heaving as he cut out the lion's tooth. What a figure of a man! Even the mighty Gilgamesh took spears, bows and arrows, and a battle axe when he went lion hunting, along with ten of his bravest guards, similarly equipped.

Enkidu killed lions bare-handed.

"My mighty one," she mouthed. Enkidu's size, his strength, his innocence, the way he risked his life to save the sheep made her long for him to come to her bed again. When they arrived in Uruk, he would make the city men look like scheming eunuchs. Enkidu was exactly what the city needed: someone who could defeat Gilgamesh and free the people from his overbearing rule.

She dug her fingers into the wool blanket. Zaidu was a thinker, a planner, a reliable man. Enkidu was none of those. He was a glutton for physical pleasures and could barely speak. He was much like Gilgamesh himself.

"You stare at him so," Zaidu said as the shepherds went to thank Enkidu and exclaim over the lion.

"He doesn't belong in Uruk. I wrong him by taking him to the city."

"He's a man. He doesn't belong with the gazelles either."

"He fits in nowhere."

"He is a good shepherd. If not for him, Adapa and Hanzamu would be dead, as well as some sheep. He could stay with them." Zaidu looked away. "You should stay too."

He assumed she would choose him. She was not so sure.

The next morning, Shamhat woke knowing she couldn't allow her sympathy for Enkidu's plight to interfere with her goal. Despite his animal manners and not-quite-right appearance, Enkidu was human and belonged in a city.

After dressing and combing her hair, she left her tent for the cooking fire. Enkidu sat next to it, gobbling down bread. She knelt in the sand next to him. "Enkidu, it's time I told you about the Gods' plans for you." Zaidu turned his head slightly, although he continued rubbing salt on the hide of the ewe the lion had killed.

Enkidu looked from one shepherd to another, his cheeks bulging with bread. "Which shepherd 'Gods'?"

Shamhat sighed at how much he still needed to learn. "Gods are not humans. They look like humans, and They eat bread and drink beer like humans. They get married and have families like humans. But They live forever. The Gods created humans to grow Their food."

Enkidu showed no interest.

"The king of Uruk, the head male, sent me here to find you. King Gilgamesh is the greatest king in the world, huge and strong and handsome, and he wants to meet you."

"Is he strong like me? Kill he lions?"

"Not like you, but—"

"I better man. I go to Uruk. I show."

"The king had a dream. He saw a bright star cross the bowl of heaven and land at his feet as a giant stone. Gilgamesh's mother told him the dream meant he would meet a dear friend and mighty hero, a companion of his heart. The king believes you're this friend.

"But Enkidu, a king should be like a shepherd to his people, protecting and guiding them. Gilgamesh is a bad shepherd to the citizens of Uruk the Sheepfold. The people cry to the Gods to help them."

Enkidu blinked. "Why bad shepherd?"

Shamhat mentally ran through Gilgamesh's sins. She doubted Enkidu would sympathize with the young men forced to run races. But she did know one story that would stir his liver. "There was a girl, a young girl, who had never lain with a man. Her father gave her to a husband who promised to take care of her. But Gilgamesh forced himself on her. She cried in fear and pain, but he didn't stop. He hurt her badly."

Enkidu jumped to his feet, his face red and a blood vessel in his neck pulsing. "I go Uruk now. I challenge Gilgamesh. I show who best man."

The shepherds cheered. "That's the spirit!" Adapa shouted.

Shamhat stood and held up her hands. "Enough! Enkidu is not yet ready for the city. He needs to hear of the other dream.

"The *en*-priest of Inanna, the Goddess of love, also had a dream. In his dream, farmers planned a great feast for the harvest." Shamhat told Enkidu the rest of the dream. "King Gilgamesh is the man who ruined the fields and beer. You, Enkidu, are the great bull aurochs who rescues the farmers."

Zaidu wiped his brow. "How can both the king's dream and the *en*-priest's be true?"

Hanzamu said, with great confidence, "One dream came from the spirits, and the other didn't." The other shepherds murmured agreement.

"Which dream is which?" Zaidu asked. It was a question Shamhat had avoided thinking about. "Will Enkidu be Gilgamesh's friend or enemy?"

Enkidu thumped his fists against his chest. "I go Uruk. I challenge Gilgamesh. I show who best man."

"Finish your meal." Shamhat handed Enkidu a *kuli* of beer. "We'll go to Uruk later."

"Beer!" Enkidu slurped from the *kuli* and wandered off toward the sheepfold.

Fear gripped Shamhat's throat. She knew the dream sent by Inanna to Her *en*-priest was the true one. Yet Enkidu was so trusting and easily swayed, and Gilgamesh could be so charming. Could Enkidu's path be perverted?

Chapter 15: Goodbyes

The wilderness
A week later
Shamhat

AS THE SHEPHERDS JOKED AND THEIR WIVES CLEARED up after the morning meal, Shamhat tried to figure out a way to interrupt Zaidu. He sat cross-legged with a large piece of leather over his thigh. He rested a chunk of flint on the leather and struck it repeatedly with an egg-shaped piece of limestone. A thick, hand-long length of wild boar tusk lay next to him, along with a knife and an arrow point he had already finished. His face had an intense look of concentration, and chips of stone flew about as he worked.

Enkidu was ready to go to Uruk. Shamhat had spent dawn to dusk with him the past week, teaching him words, prayers, and the names and duties of the Gods. She had described the glories of Uruk—the many-fingered *Buranun*, the boats that carried people from one place to another, the glowing white temple of An, the baked-brick city wall, the cool gardens of palms and fruit trees, the people singing and dancing in the street during the many festivals. Each morning when he came back from the sheepfold, she took him to her bed. Each day he depended on her more and grew more eager for Uruk. Today they would leave.

"Zaidu?"

He jerked, and his hammerstone cracked away a quarter of the flint. Shamhat flinched. "I'm sorry."

He stared at the flint. "What do you want?"

"I wanted to ask you one last time to come with us."

"You don't need me to protect you when you have Enkidu." His voice was bitter. He put the broken-off chunk of flint to the side and started flaking the main piece of flint.

"You and your father would be better off in the city. Life is easier, and food is plentiful."

"And your vow of chastity—will you break it for me as you did for Enkidu?"

Shamhat drew back as if slapped. "Walk with me."

"There isn't any more to say." He wrapped his tools and stones in the leather and got up anyway. He walked fast, like a merchant late for a meeting with a client. Once they were out of earshot of the shepherds and Enkidu, she placed her hand on his arm. He glared at her hand but left it there.

"I can't break my vow for you. Inanna has rules. The vow of chastity is lifted only at New Year's and only for the priestess who reenacts with the king the sacred marriage of Inanna and Dumuzi." Her gaze slid away. She had to tell him the rest of it. "And even if I could, to control Enkidu, I'll have to keep him in my bed."

"You can't break your vow for me, but you do for Enkidu." Zaidu spat like a goat, and his voice roughened. "Enkidu would happily couple with any woman in Uruk and not know the difference. He'd as soon run through Uruk's streets with the pigs as be with you."

Shamhat's cheeks grew hot. "I'm doing what I must. You started this, asking the king for help with the wild man."

"What will happen when the king or the *en*-priest finds out how you tamed Enkidu?"

Shamhat's chest tightened. "If I am doing Inanna's will, She will protect me." Tears welled in her eyes, and she blinked them back. "Who would I be if I were not a priestess of Inanna? No one."

"*Ashe!*" Zaidu sat and pulled her down next to him. "You act as if the world is at stake."

"It is." Shamhat clasped her cold hands together. "Gods are capricious. They could decide to destroy Uruk to punish Gilgamesh. They could decide to destroy the world. They did it once before, with a great flood. I have to take Enkidu back and he must humble Gilgamesh."

"You speak passionately, as if Gilgamesh harmed you personally."

She turned her head away. "The young girl I told Enkidu about? The one Gilgamesh raped? She's my brother's wife." Zaidu hissed, and tears clogged Shamhat's nose and kept her from speaking for several moments. "When my brother threatened to kill the king, I promised to find a way to humble Gilgamesh. Our family would be disgraced and destroyed if Geshtu tried to take revenge. Then when the king ordered me to find and bring back Enkidu, he took my son hostage. So I risk losing him, too, if I don't return with Enkidu."

"Your life would be easier here. Stay."

She imagined a life in the desert. She would miss city luxuries, yes, and she would grow old young, as the shepherds' wives did. But she wouldn't miss bearing the burden of seventy thousand lives. She sighed. "I can't. For the sake of my son and my brother and Uruk, I must take Enkidu to the city."

Zaidu kissed her roughly, once, then pulled her to her feet. "I can't go with you. I couldn't bear to see you with Enkidu, knowing he lies with you. Besides, *Ada* and I would be as dependent on you as Enkidu is. We would distract you and endanger your family."

Shamhat stared out across the desert. "I was selfish to want a friend with me. Any shame or punishment should fall only on me." Her shoulders and back were tight, and her head ached.

"You can come back here, afterwards."

"I belong in the city, as you belong in the desert."

"Do you really believe it's that simple?"

She had no answer.

On the trip from Uruk, Shamhat had found the desert monotonous, foreign, bleak, a wasteland made more unbearable by the cloudless sky that let the full force of the sun glare on the burning sand. After living there for weeks, she saw the desert differently. The dunes now undulated with light and shadow under the lapis lazuli sky.

This time she noticed the plants the sheep grazed on in the rainy season, the vultures patrolling overhead and the jackals below, and the scuttling of scorpions, sand crickets, dung beetles, and other creatures nearby. She wished she could tell Zaidu she saw a worm lizard peek out of its burrow.

"We go too slow," Enkidu complained before noon on the first day.

"My legs are much shorter than yours." Shamhat already panted from the pace.

"Then I carry you."

And he did, for hours at a time, running across the sand with Shamhat on his back like a small child, clinging to his neck and back, her hair tangling in the wind.

At meals and before they went to bed, Shamhat told Enkidu about Gilgamesh and the innocents he had hurt. She reminded him that he needed to challenge Gilgamesh to prove himself the better man. She described the many kinds of beer made in the city. Before they went to sleep, she used all the skills of Inanna to pleasure him and bind him to her.

They reached the north gate of Uruk on the morning of the third day.

Chapter 16: Battle of Titans

Uruk
That morning
Enkidu, Shamhat

ENKIDU STEPPED FROM WHAT SHAMHAT CALLED A "BOAT" onto what she called a "dock." He stood tall, head high and hands on his hips. Shamhat placed her hand inside his elbow and whispered to him, telling him what he saw. The wall before them stretched higher than the tallest tree. They headed toward a small opening at the bottom, the "gates."

Enkidu had to duck to fit through. When he straightened, his mouth dropped open. Humans and donkeys and pigs swarmed everywhere like vermin on a dead body. People wore the skins of sheep. He wrinkled his nose in disgust.

So many smells, so close. River. Barley. Scented oil. He swayed, dizzy. His eyes could not make sense of what he saw. His ears rang from the shouting and braying and singing and clanging.

"*Alala!*" Shamhat knelt and kissed the dirt. "Lady Inanna, I am glad to be back in Your city."

Short, scrawny humans ran up to touch Enkidu's skirt and darted away, giggling. One came forward again and thrust out its chest boldly. "What are you? A giant?"

Shamhat answered. "This is Enkidu, a hero from the desert and a killer of lions. He has come to visit King Gilgamesh." Shamhat stood on her toes and whispered in his ear, "These are boys, young males."

Among the gazelles, the adults started out as small, weak younglings. "Will they be gazelles when they grow up?"

"No, they'll be men. The girls—the young females—will be women, like me."

The bold boy giggled. "We'll take you to the king. Three rings of silver."

"Bah!" Shamhat said. "We're not country bumpkins. Some barley for each of you would be enough. But I have other tasks that *are* worth silver." She took two shiny rings from her basket and held them out toward the boy. "Send a boy to the shops to buy me sandals, a beaded sash, and a ribbon for my hair. Send another to Geshtu the cylinder-seal maker who lives near Kirum's tavern and tell him his sister is home."

The boy took the rings. He told two other boys what to do. They ran away in different directions. The leader boy drew himself up proudly. He shouted, "Make way! Make way for King Enkidu the Lion Killer!"

"Lion-Killer! Lion-Killer!" the remaining boys chanted.

Enkidu pounded on his chest. Shamhat tugged on his arm. "Come. Let everyone admire your beauty and strength." He walked with her. Many people came to him, placing their hands on his lion skin or his arm. Some stretched on tiptoe to touch his beard or knelt to kiss his feet. Shamhat smiled. "They already recognize your greatness."

A mountain loomed over the city, and the boys led them toward it. Shamhat pointed to the mountain. "That is the temple of An."

"Noisy." Enkidu covered his ears. "I don't like."

"There's a parade ahead." Shamhat stood on her tiptoes. "Can you see it yet?"

The boy led them around a building, and Enkidu stopped. People lined the paths, and the smell of beer made his mouth water. Women with painted faces danced. Men clanged round shiny things. On a boat in the canal rode a huge man, completely still, his face shining like the sun and his garments gleaming with colored rocks. Flowers lay around the man's feet. "Gilgamesh!" Enkidu shouted. He fisted his hands and pushed past the boy.

Shamhat grabbed him. "No, that's Utu, God of the sun and justice, Gilgamesh's personal God. It's a festival day, and Utu's going visiting." She turned to the boy. "Can you find us a way around the parade?" The boy held out his hand. Shamhat gave him a small bread they had gotten in a village last night.

A boy ran to Shamhat and gave her a basket. Shamhat put garments on her feet. The head boy led them back the way they had come and down another path and then another. Enkidu was lost. But Shamhat always knew where they were and told him stories about the businesses and people, stories he did not understand. "What's a butcher?"

"Butchers kill sheep and cattle and other animals and cut them into parts for people to eat."

"They are murderers?"

Shamhat dropped her basket in surprise. "Don't you eat the creatures of the earth, Enkidu? The Gods created them as food."

Enkidu wrinkled his nose. "I eat crickets and ants and other creeping things. But the grass-eaters are my brothers and sisters. I will kill Gilgamesh for allowing butchers."

The boy turned down yet another path. "*Ashe!*" Shamhat called as she tied a yellow garment with colored rocks on it around her waist. "This isn't the way to the king's great house."

"There's a wedding feast going on. The king is visiting the bride." He pointed.

Enkidu's followed the line of the boy's finger. Outside one of the mud-brick buildings stood a man of such grandness and beauty he knew at once it was Gilgamesh.

Roaring, he charged.

Shamhat ran after Enkidu, twisting her hair and tying it up with an embroidered ribbon. The wedding was at the house of Lu-Dingir-Ra the perfume maker. This day would decide the future of Uruk and of Shamhat and her family. Either Gilgamesh would kill Enkidu, or Enkidu would kill Gilgamesh.

Gilgamesh turned and seemed to grow larger as Enkidu bore down on him. "Kneel to your king!" Gilgamesh cried. Enkidu crashed into him, smashing him against Lu-Dingir-Ra's house. Gilgamesh grabbed Enkidu's arms and butted his head against Enkidu's. The two staggered into the street, howling like wild beasts as they grappled.

Lu-Dingir-Ra, his daughter, and his wedding guests in their finery ran out of the house, babbling. The combatants ignored them and the other people who ran from neighboring houses and streets. Gilgamesh and Enkidu crashed heads again with a fearsome crack, and Gilgamesh shoved Enkidu to the ground. Enkidu leapt up with his gazelle-like speed, picked Gilgamesh up, and threw him against a wall. Spectators screamed as the house shook and the door posts fell into the street.

Gilgamesh pushed away from the house and ripped off his robe. Sweat poured down his face and chest, but he was smiling. He ran at Enkidu, grabbed him by his lion skin, and spun him around. When he let go, Enkidu stumbled several steps and fell to his knees. But as Gilgamesh threw himself at Enkidu, the wild man rolled away and to his feet.

Gilgamesh rose and feinted to the left, then lunged and wrapped his arms around his opponent. For the first time, Shamhat could compare them as fighters. Gilgamesh stood a hand's-width taller, but Enkidu had bigger bones and longer arms. Gilgamesh knew the standard moves of wrestling and fighting, but Enkidu had the strength and speed of a man who had run with gazelles.

Shamhat had hoped Enkidu would have the advantage, but they were evenly matched. "Great Inanna, help Your champion. Queen of Heaven, take pity on Your city and its people." The giants grappled, neither letting go, staggering this way and that, the crowd running back and forth to find a good view while staying clear of the fight.

The men crashed into the wall of another house, and their combined weight, that of two lionesses, cracked the bricks. Shamhat winced. Both men were smeared with dust and blood.

Vendors arrived, skirting the mêlée. "Beer here!" "Dried fish!" "Pressed-date bread!"

Geshtu ran to her, puffing and holding his sides. "You look terrible, Shamhat!" He grabbed her in a bear hug.

"Good health to you, too, brother." She squeezed him back and then gestured toward the fight. "I told you I'd find a way to humble

Gilgamesh and avenge his insult to you. Behold Inanna's champion, Enkidu."

Geshtu whistled to a bread vendor and bought two flat breads. He held one out to her. "Who's winning?"

Shamhat waved the bread away and wrapped her arms around herself, her guts tightening. "I don't know." The men fought on, longer than it seemed possible for men to fight, and the crowd grew. Shamhat's stomach threatened to empty, and she shuddered and winced with each buffet and blow. At last, Gilgamesh pulled free of Enkidu. The men staggered apart and glared at each other. Then they threw themselves at each other again. Gilgamesh caught Enkidu in a wrestling move, threw him to the ground, and dropped, pinning Enkidu to the ground with his knee.

A hush fell over the crowd. Shamhat's hands flew to her mouth. *Throw him off, Enkidu,* she thought. *Get up! Get up!* The two contestants' breathing rasped, but she held her breath.

"You are the greater." Enkidu tipped his head back like a dog yielding to its better.

Shamhat turned and fell against Geshtu, who steadied her. "*Meliea!* I have failed! Who will save us now from the tyrant?"

Chapter 17: The Star That Fell From Heaven

Uruk
Noon that same day
Gilgamesh

GILGAMESH FELT AS IF UTU HAD LIFTED HIM into the sky. Joy replaced his rage, and happiness his despair. "*Alala!*" he shouted, throwing his hands toward the sun. "Utu, truly You are the greatest of all Gods."

He climbed off his opponent and held out his hand to help him up. Each studied the other's face. Gilgamesh remembered his dream of a star that streamed light across the bowl of heaven and fell to his feet as a boulder. This man's eyes shone like stars, his brows curved like the bowl of heaven, and his muscles were angled and hard like boulders. His liver told him this man was the one his mother had called his double, his second self.

The man tipped his head and offered his neck like a chastened dog. "Gilgamesh, you are greater than all other humans. You deserve to rule the greatest city."

Gilgamesh looked at the two lion teeth that hung from a cord around the man's neck. "I sent the priestess Shamhat into the desert to find a wild man. Are you he?"

"I was." The man hung his head. "Now I am Enkidu."

Gilgamesh's chest threatened to burst with pity. "I'll make you happy to be human." He opened wide his arms. "We shall be as brothers."

They embraced, this time as companions instead of combatants, and Gilgamesh kissed Enkidu on the lips. "Walk by my side as an equal," Gilgamesh pleaded. "Come, live in my big house. I will give you a room and a wife. You'll wear garments of the finest linen and wool, and I'll adorn you with jewels. For us, every day will be a festival."

Enkidu smiled, an innocent, joyous smile unlike any Gilgamesh had ever seen. A strange emotion overtook him, and it took him a moment to recognize it.

Peace.

Gilgamesh closed his eyes and luxuriated in the simple joy of being Gilgamesh, king of Uruk, standing in the city he ruled. For once, he was not driven to do or be anything else. "You've calmed my restless *zi*, Enkidu. Truly, the Gods sent you to me." Gilgamesh held Enkidu's hand like a brother, and together they walked home.

Chapter 18: Plots and Schemes

Uruk
Early afternoon
Shamhat

"YOU FAILED," GESHTU SNAPPED.

"Inanna forgive me." Shamhat's limbs felt like heavy stones, and her stomach tightened in worry. She rested her forehead in her hands. "I must fetch Inanna-Ama-Mu from the king's house. I must go to the temple. I must—"

"Calm yourself," Geshtu interrupted. "Get Inanna-Ama-Mu, but then come home. We must talk. The temple can wait."

Her duty to the temple came first, but Shamhat nodded in agreement anyway. She could not yet bear to admit her failure to Nanna-Ur-Sag. As Geshtu walked away, she spotted a sliver of shade next to a two-story house. She needed to paint her face and retie her sash and hair ribbon before she went to the king's great house, or the Wife of Gilgamesh would take insult.

Despite her fatigue and despair, she hurried to the king's house as fast as dignity allowed. A guard barred her entry to the courtyard with his spear. "Who are you and what do you want?"

"Babati, don't you recognize me? It's Shamhat, priestess of Inanna."

He peered closer, then straightened to attention. "Forgive me, my lady. You look . . . different." He stepped aside.

She gave him one of her Inanna smiles. "Thank you for saying 'different' and not 'terrible.'"

"You went into the wilderness on the king's business. I honor and admire your bravery." He bowed stiffly, then relaxed and smiled. "Your boy's well."

She took in a deep breath her chest had been too tight to draw before. "Thank you for telling me." She scurried through the doorway and took the passageway past a room in which men shouted in laughter. In the open-air personal courtyard, surrounded by singing birds in hanging cages, the Wife of Gilgamesh sat on a bench under a reed overhang, dictating a letter to a scribe asking for a report from the manager of her weaving workshop, one of her many businesses. Her two young sons, Ur-Nungal and Amar-Utu, tumbled with Inanna-Ama-Mu, punching and kicking and yelping. The wetnurse held back the king's toddler daughter, who stretched pudgy arms toward the playing boys.

Shamhat stopped at the edge of the courtyard. The Wife of Gilgamesh motioned her in and told the scribe to wait. "They're all so much like their father, aren't they? Although Inanna-Ama-Mu knows enough to hold back. He fights only hard enough to win." She looked at Shamhat's face. "You look tired. You may sit."

"Thank you, great lady." Shamhat sank to her knees next to the bench, welcoming the rest. "At his age, Inanna-Ama-Mu should know enough to let the king's heirs win. Political skill is a trait he'll need when he's a priest." The Wife of Gilgamesh smiled smugly. As often as possible, Shamhat acknowledged that Gilgamesh's oldest son would never be king. It seemed the best course to keep Inanna-Ama-Mu safe from assassins.

"Your trip succeeded." The Wife of Gilgamesh tipped her head toward the raucous laughing Shamhat had passed and made a wry face. "The wild man appears to like beer."

"Very much. And bread too. Enkidu has learned that much of civilization. But after living with grazing animals, he refuses to eat any. In fact, he became angry when we passed a butcher shop and I explained what a butcher does."

"I'll tell the kitchen staff." The Wife of Gilgamesh looked at Inanna-Ama-Mu. "Are you here to take him?"

"He's no longer a hostage, is he?" Shamhat asked carefully and respectfully. "I did do everything the king asked of me."

"Hostage? Oh, you misunderstood." Her cold expression contradicted her words. "You may have him, and you may leave." She motioned to a basket in the corner. "I had a servant gather his things."

"Thank you, Great Lady." Shamhat walked into the pile of boys and grabbed the biggest one by an ear. "Inanna-Ama-Mu, it's time for you to return to the temple. Bow to the Wife of Gilgamesh."

"Ow!" he shrieked, then grinned at her. She restrained the urge to wrap her arms around him and press him to her bosom, to kiss his head, to pick him up and swing him around the room.

Instead, she took his hand and led him out of the king's great house. She walked as slowly as she could, asking about his lessons and his progress, listening to his tales of pranks and his complaints about the stern *nin*-priestess. She stopped at shops along the way, buying him a sash threaded with gold and a toy sheep carved from precious cedar.

Too soon, they reached the temple gate. "Thank you for the sheep, Lady of Inanna," he said. "You're nice. I'm glad the temple sent you to fetch me." She dared to touch his head. He ran up the stairs without a look back.

Emptiness blossomed in Shamhat's chest. She took a boat to Geshtu's house, pressing her lips together to keep from sobbing. A child born of the rite of Sacred Marriage was the son of the Goddess. Inanna-Ama-Mu did not know Shamhat had carried him in her womb, and she could never tell him.

When Shamhat reached home, a mat covered the door, even though it was early afternoon. She walked into the entrance and turned. The air cooled as she walked between the thick walls to the interior courtyard. Geshtu and Kirum sat next to each other in the corner, their faces serious and their heads close, as *Ama* wove at her loom. Half-finished cylinder seals, stone fragments, and pieces of gold foil littered Geshtu's worktable. His flint drills were dull with dust. Dabta was nowhere in sight.

"Good health." She sat on a nearby bench, sighing. "It's good to be home. But Geshtu, why aren't you working? Kirum, why aren't you at your tavern?"

Geshtu and Kirum exchanged glances. "We're planning a revolt." Geshtu's hand touched the dagger in his sash. "You're going to help us."

A cold chill went up Shamhat's back. "Gilgamesh is too powerful, and he has many guards. You'll be killed in the street like a rabid dog."

"Nameshda is no better. The physicians agree she's as well as she'll ever be." His jaw tightened and loosened several times. "They say she'll never be able to give birth."

Shamhat put her hands to her mouth. "Poor Nameshda! Does she know?"

Geshtu swallowed. "No. *Ama* begged me not to tell her."

Shamhat reached out and put her hand on his. "She'll have to be told when your new wife arrives."

Geshtu shook her hand off. "I won't let Gilgamesh hurt my family again. I won't take a second wife until the king is dead."

Shamhat started. "You'd let our family line die out? You can't!"

"Of course I can. You keep forgetting I'm now head of this household."

Shamhat looked him in the eyes and saw determination there, as well as new lines and sadness.

"Gilgamesh dishonored me and my family and hurt Nameshda." Geshtu's voice broke. "That's my fault, for marrying her when I knew Gilgamesh had ruined other brides, and it's your fault, too, Shamhat."

"Mine!"

"You didn't convince him to leave the wedding."

"It's hardly my fault he prefers to terrorize the meek and fearful."

"Don't use that tone of voice with me!"

Ama stopped working, and the house fell still.

"I'm sorry." Shamhat had to force the words out. Everywhere else, she was a priestess of Inanna, subject only to the *en*-priest and the king, but here her little brother ruled.

"This is why you must help us. To right the wrong you did, and so our family can continue."

Geshtu had always had a hot temper, but never had he carried a grudge so long. Shamhat couldn't blame him. She turned to Kirum, whose childlike face looked taut and strained. "Why do you encourage him?"

Kirum blushed. "Sagburru returned to the clay two years ago, and I want to remarry." She looked shyly at her hands. "Lulu-Numu-Al-Banti the fisherman loves me."

Kirum had never surprised her more. "Why remarry? Few women are as free as you. Why would you want a husband to rule you?"

"I'm not like you, Shamhat. I'm willing to trade my freedom for a family. All I have now are the people in this room. I go to sleep in an empty house."

"But you're afraid to remarry because of the king?"

"I don't want to go through what Nameshda went through." Kirum's face and neck turned bright red, and she hunched her shoulders around her ears.

"Again," she whispered.

The room seemed to tilt, and Shamhat grabbed the bench to steady herself. Kirum came to sit next to her, and Shamhat hugged her. "You never told me."

"You were half in love with Gilgamesh after the Sacred Marriage rite." Kirum's voice choked. "Besides, I wanted to have at least one friend who didn't know my shame." She leaned against Shamhat's shoulder and sobbed.

Geshtu shifted in obvious embarrassment. "If the wronged men unite, we will have more fighters than the king. Kirum's tavern is the perfect recruiting spot. We already have the perfect assassin, someone welcome at the king's great house."

The knot in Shamhat's stomach tightened. "Who would so dare defy the Gods?"

"You."

"No!" Shamhat's palms grew clammy, and she shivered. "Gilgamesh must be punished, yes. But this great sin is not the way! The Gods would destroy us and Uruk."

Geshtu pounded his fist in his hand. "There is no other way!"

"Give me time. Give me more time." Shamhat twisted her finger in her hair, her thoughts desperate and racing. "Inanna's plan for Enkidu to humble the king may have failed today. But Enkidu is now living with the king. He'll have more chances. I'll whisper in his ear."

"How many more young men will the king injure while we wait? How many more brides will he despoil?" Geshtu struck the bench with his fist. "We must act now. We've already waited for you once."

"Please." Shamhat knelt before her little brother and put her forehead on the dirt floor. "Give me another chance. Wouldn't you rather see him humiliated than dead?"

Kirum spoke vehemently. "I would. I would give much to see him shamed."

Unexpectedly, *Ama* spoke. "Geshtu, don't you have faith in your sister?"

Shamhat dared to look at Geshtu. He sucked in his cheeks, and his fists loosened. "We have waited so long already, we can wait a little longer. But if your wild man doesn't deliver, you must do as I say."

Still shaking, Shamhat headed on foot for the Eanna, tripping several times. She should have taken a boat. She kept her head down so no one would recognize her and think a priestess was publicly drunk. When she arrived, she went first to the bathhouse and then to the dormitory to wrap herself in a clean shawl, paint her face, and put on some jewelry. The routine calmed her. Now she could report to the *en*-priest.

She found him on the second level of the temple watching the distribution of the remains of Inanna's meal to the poor who had gathered below. Again she fell to her knees and pressed her forehead to the ground. "Good health to you, my lord. I regret to report I have failed."

"Good health, daughter." He placed his hand on her head. "Let's talk in private. I want to hear about this Enkidu." She stood and followed him to the cella. She repeated her obeisance before Inanna and then stood next to one of the carved alabaster vases.

Nanna-Ur-Sag studied her, looking, she knew, for any sign of discomposure. But though her entire body ached from exhaustion, and her guts writhed, she kept her brow calm, her hands relaxed, and her posture regal. "Good," he said. "Your training is intact, despite your time in the wilderness. But your eyes have aged." His gazed flicked to the spot on her chest where her cylinder seal should hang, but he did not comment on its absence, only handed her the choker of lapis lazuli beads the city guard had taken. "When Inanna descended to the Netherworld, she gave up all her symbols of status and power. You seem to have made a similar journey."

Shamhat could not read the *en*-priest's mood. He did not seem angry; rather, he seemed contemplative and sad. "Nanna-Ur-Sag, the temple is my life. I've been here since I was twelve. You've been a second father to me, and the priestesses have been my sisters. Please do not make me leave."

He put his hand on her shoulder. "You've admitted no wrongdoing, and no one has complained of you. What is this talk of leaving?"

"But—" Shamhat stopped, confused. He knew how the king had expected her to tame Enkidu.

Nanna-Ur-Sag abruptly changed the subject. "Gilgamesh defeated the wild man. Is the city doomed?"

Shamhat's heart slowed its furious pounding. "Enkidu may yet humble the king."

"Tell me about Enkidu."

"He's a child in a man's body."

Nanna-Ur-Sag went to Inanna and stiffly knelt to polish the copper toes she wore. "How so?"

"He's impulsive and never considers consequences. He pouts when he doesn't get his way. He brags about his strength and size. He won't sit still, drinks too much, and can't control his temper."

"Traits that sometimes describe our king. What are Enkidu's good qualities? Can we use him against Gilgamesh?"

"Yes, I think so." She should not stand uselessly by while the *en*-priest labored. She took the fringed edge of her shawl and brushed dust from the crevices and intricate curves of Inanna's jewelry. "Enkidu is a champion of the helpless, and he's incredibly strong. Without any weapons, he killed a lion to protect some sheep. When I told him how Gilgamesh abuses the brides, he got angry and wanted to come to Uruk to teach the king a lesson."

"Yet I heard he and Gilgamesh walked off to the great house hand in hand."

"True. But what will Enkidu do when he sees Gilgamesh harm his citizens? Will his pride let him stay in Gilgamesh's shadow?" She swallowed. "The people I mentioned before—they still want to overthrow the king." She would not tell him she spoke of her brother and her best friend, but it would be easy enough to guess. She had to hope he would keep it quiet.

"Are you and Enkidu friends?"

"Yes." She smiled, thinking of their trip to Uruk, her riding on his back as he ran across the desert yelping with joy.

"Then play on that. Visit him, praise him, and keep him your friend." He looked up from Inanna's shining toes. "You may go now. You need some rest."

Shamhat hugged her arms to her chest. They hadn't discussed the most important matter of all. "What happens to me?"

Nanna-Ur-Sag stopped polishing and sat on his heels. "People may whisper about your role in taming Enkidu. I'd like you to be inconspicuous for a while—work on your hymns, update the accounts, visit Enkidu discreetly. I'll assume you're unstained, and I won't ask you outright. We'll wait and pray. But if you become pregnant, I'll have no choice."

Shamhat squeezed her eyes shut, and her headache returned full force. If she proved impure, the *en*-priest would have to turn her out of the temple in disgrace.

Chapter 19: Enkidu the Magnificent

Uruk
The next morning
Gilgamesh

L AUGHING, GILGAMESH RAN TO THE GATE, Enkidu by his side. Babati stepped forward, his bald head glistening. "Lord King, your council of young men is waiting in the public courtyard." He glanced at Gilgamesh's sweaty, naked chest. "What would you like me to tell them?"

Gilgamesh slapped his forehead and groaned. He'd completely forgotten he had called a meeting for this morning. He had taken Enkidu on an early morning walk to show him his kingdom, and they had raced back. He had won, but it had been a challenge, a welcome challenge.

Enkidu stomped his foot. "You promised to show me the river gate."

"And I'll show it to you. Babati, please give the young men my apologies and an arm's length of wool each."

"The Wife of Gilgamesh also humbly begs you to visit her at your convenience. Your older son is sick, and she wants your opinion on the physician's advice."

"Tell her I trust her judgement."

"Yes, Lord King." Babati went back to his station.

"Ready to see the river gate now?" Gilgamesh asked Enkidu, marveling that he could look at him without lowering his head. Enkidu had intriguing eyes. His gaze darted about like a wild gazelle's, always on the lookout, although Enkidu's eyes were bold, not fearful.

"Yes!"

"I challenge you to find it on your own." Gilgamesh had already learned Enkidu delighted in games as much as he did.

Enkidu tipped his head back and slowly turned in a circle, sniffing noisily. Then he broke into a trot toward the river, his bulky back and calf muscles bunching and stretching. Gilgamesh maintained an easy pace behind him, joyful that he ran for pleasure, not because his *zi* made him. His mind was a quiet pool. He watched the citizens make way for Enkidu as if he were also a king, and he saw their admiring glances. Already the citizens gave Enkidu their respect.

Enkidu found the *Buranun* and followed it downriver until he reached the city wall. He blinked, and Gilgamesh laughed at his surprise. "The river continues on the other side," Gilgamesh said, slapping him on the back, "but we have to tell the guards to open the gate."

Enkidu gave him a wide grin and pelted past the rude reed-and-mud huts lining the river. When he reached the wall, he jumped and caught hold of a brick set unevenly. Gilgamesh held his breath as Enkidu dangled. Then Enkidu found footholds and climbed. The guards at the gate cheered him on. When he reached the top, he waved and ran to the other side and out of sight.

Gilgamesh had never scaled the wall, had never considered it, but he would not be upstaged.

A screech interrupted his thoughts. "Lord King, Lord King, I have a complaint against Imgal the butcher." The old woman held out a bundle wrapped in reeds. "Look at this!" She folded back the reeds and lifted off the top piece of meat. The piece underneath wriggled with worms.

Gilgamesh's temper flared. "That's disgraceful! This Imgal must be punished." His fists opened and closed. Selling bad goods and using false weights and measures were serious offenses. He would not tolerate cheats in his city. "Where is Imgal's shop?"

"This way, Lord King." The woman walked away.

Gilgamesh followed for a few steps and then remembered. Enkidu awaited him. "Go to your district councilman," he called to the woman. "He'll help you." As she protested, Gilgamesh ran for the wall. It took him three tries, but Enkidu couldn't see him, so they didn't count. He clambered up the wall and sat on top. Uruk looked different from here. Only An's temple topped the wall. The *Buranun* and its canals and tributaries dominated the city, and gardens took up a third of the city.

He stood and walked across the broad top of the wall, thicker than most of the canals were wide. Enkidu waved from below. Sunlight flashed off the river, and snatches of the songs of traders and boatmen reached him. He stretched and sighed. Uruk was a great city, and it was his, all of it. Now that he had Enkidu, he would put city business aside and take time to enjoy his treasures.

Chapter 20: Jealousy

Uruk
Two weeks later
Shamhat, Gilgamesh

DEPRIVED OF THE COMFORT OF THE DAILY ROUTINE of a priestess, Shamhat created one. Four times a day, she prayed to Inanna to protect Uruk and not punish it for the king's sins. She prayed for Her to protect Zaidu, his father, and the shepherds. And she prayed for herself, too, that she did not carry Enkidu's child, despite her poor appetite and constant queasiness.

Mornings, she went to her brother's house. She helped *Ama* with Nameshda's care, talked with Geshtu about a design for her new cylinder seal, and visited Kirum before the tavern opened. Geshtu grudgingly told her he had heard no accounts of Gilgamesh raping brides or forcing men to fight or race since Enkidu arrived in the city. Kirum reported her patrons said the same. Still, the citizens remained on edge, and Inanna received more gifts from worshippers than usual.

Afternoons, Shamhat returned to the temple to attend to her scribal duties and write praise poems. After catching up on work that had accumulated while she was gone, she had time nearly every afternoon to write.

Four times, Shamhat had gone to visit Enkidu, and four times she had been turned away. Enkidu and the king were always out together—tavern hopping, lion hunting, racing in the streets. So she was surprised two weeks after Enkidu's arrival when he visited her, led to the scribes' chamber by a new slave who didn't yet know guests weren't allowed in the work areas of the temple.

118

"Enkidu!" Her liver quickened to see him. "Good health!"

He swept her up in his arms and hugged her tightly. He felt larger than she remembered. "Why don't you visit me?" he complained. "I miss you." He kissed her mouth, and Shamhat pushed him away, aware of the other scribes.

"I did visit you. You were never home." Shamhat smoothed her braid self-consciously. "Why are you alone today?"

Enkidu grimaced. "The old men said Gilgamesh must meet with them to prepare for flood season. Every day they came, and today Gilgamesh gave in. He shouldn't. He can fight them all and win."

"But Enkidu, that's what kings do—meet with the council of old men, meet with the council of young men, receive ambassadors from other cities, visit the shrines to honor the Gods and give them gifts, judge disputes, maintain the shrines and temples. You've seen how busy he is."

"No." Enkidu roamed the room, picking up and putting down tools and clay until the scribes pulled them close. "We spend every day having fun. Today, you and I have fun. Where is your bed?" He grabbed for her breasts, and a young scribe-in-training giggled.

"Everyone, out!" Shamhat ordered, feeling her face flush. The scribes picked up their work and left, the giggly one looking sideways at Enkidu from under her charcoal-lined eyelids.

If Gilgamesh neglected his duties because of Enkidu, the city was worse off than before. Panic rose in her chest. "Everyone must work, Enkidu." Her voice came out harsh. "That's why the Gods created us, so They wouldn't have to. You must allow the king to do his job. You wouldn't want someone hurt as the result of your play, would you?"

Enkidu crinkled his face in confusion. "I wouldn't hurt."

"Not directly, I know. You're a good shepherd." Enkidu's face brightened at her praise. Shamhat continued in a stern voice. "But when you keep the king from his duties, everyone suffers."

Enkidu blinked. Shamhat sighed. Enkidu clearly didn't understand. Shamhat pointed to the tablets on her table. "My job is to keep records in clay. If I didn't keep a count of the priestesses and temple workers, the cooks wouldn't know how much food to buy. If I didn't write down the praise poems, we might forget them."

Enkidu scratched his stomach, looking frustrated. "Birds make these tracks?"

"No, I make the marks. Like this." She picked up a stylus and pricked three syllables into the clay. "I just wrote your name. En-ki-du." She pointed her stylus at each syllable as she said it.

His eyes lit up. He must have understood something. "More!" he said, pointing to a tablet she had not yet taken out in the sun to dry. "What's that say?"

"Lust and love, war and death, all are Yours, great Lady."

"How about this one?" He pointed to the tablet she was working on.

Embarrassment and excitement entwined within her. "You can't tell anyone about this one," she whispered. With shaking hands she picked up the tablet and read.

"Like Inanna's reed doorpost, upright and tall is he.

"Like Inanna, he protects the weak.

"Like Inanna, he is great in anger.

"Like Inanna, he is great in love.

"Like Inanna, he rides the lion.

"His strength is like a God's; his beauty, like a God's—"

Enkidu snatched the tablet from her hand and threw it against the wall. "Who is this man you love?" he bellowed. "Tell me. I will kill him."

Shamhat swayed like grass in the wind. "Who among mortals rides the lion, Enkidu? Only you."

He pulled her to him, nudged the table off her woven reed mat, and took her there on the floor.

All the while she whispered in his ear. "You are like a God. No man can compare with you. Gilgamesh is a boy next to you, Enkidu. Gilgamesh is the shepherd of Uruk-the-Sheepfold, but who is the better shepherd? You, Enkidu, you."

"Me," he grunted. "Me."

The next morning, the limestone floor and the plastered walls shone white with the light filtering into the bedroom from the courtyard. Gilgamesh shook Enkidu's shoulder. "Wake up!" he whispered so he would not wake his wife, sleeping on his other side. "Today we fight with poles of cedars to see who is the greater."

"No, brother of my heart. Today I teach your sons to run like gazelles."

Gilgamesh stroked Enkidu's cheek. "I want you by my side always."

"But you have duties. I keep you from them."

Gilgamesh's temper raged like a wild boar, and he shook Enkidu by the arm. "Someone has poured poison in your ear! Who turned you against me? Who?"

His lady jolted awake. "My lord, what's wrong? Why are you shouting?"

"Someone wants to separate Enkidu and me." For a moment, he thought he saw fear in his lady's eyes, but when he blinked, it was gone.

"Only a traitor would cross the king Inanna has given them." She grabbed her shawl from the floor and wrapped it about her.

"A traitor!" Gilgamesh repeated. He ground his teeth together. "Who is the traitor who has taken advantage of your innocence, Enkidu? Name him, I command it."

"Don't be angry." Enkidu's eyes brightened with tears, and he grasped the lion teeth hanging on his chest. "Shamhat said—"

"Shamhat! She's jealous because I took you from her."

His lady touched Gilgamesh on his shoulder. "Perhaps, my lord, you should find out what the priestess said. If she is a traitor, you need to know."

"Shamhat serves the will of Inanna and her king. She's no traitor."

His wife rubbed against him like a cat and purred in his ear. "Shamhat has another loyalty, does she not?"

Gilgamesh nuzzled against her perfumed soft curves, so different from Enkidu's hard muscles. His wife was right. Inanna-Ama-Mu might be the son of Inanna legally, but he had grown in Shamhat's womb. She loved him as fiercely as any mother. Did she love Inanna-Ama-Mu enough to try to put him on the throne? "Enkidu, think. What did Shamhat say?"

Enkidu's ruggedly beautiful face looked bewildered. "She showed me praise poems she put on mud. She told me the Gods created humans to work. She said I keep you from the work the Gods gave you."

"Ereshkigal take her!" He and Shamhat had shared the Sacred Marriage bed in the New Year's rites, and he had believed they were friends. But she tried to keep him from his soulmate. "Enkidu, Inanna made me king and gave me the authority to rule Uruk in the manner I see fit. Shamhat cannot judge me. No one can judge me but the Gods."

Enkidu blinked.

His wife leaned across Gilgamesh's chest to speak to Enkidu. "Did she take you to her bed?"

Gilgamesh let out his breath in a hiss. The priestess would not have dared.

"No. We coupled on the floor."

"She took advantage of Enkidu's innocence," his lady said.

Jealousy bit him like a scorpion. "She must be kept from him." Gilgamesh pounded his fist on the cedar bed post, causing his wife to jump. "Wife, summon Shamhat today. Tell her to never again force her presence on Enkidu."

She bowed low, a smile on her face. "As you wish, Great Lord."

The private outdoor courtyard at the great house of Gilgamesh was empty except for birds. The caged ones continued to sing, but those in the potted palms flew away when Shamhat entered. "Wait here. The Wife of Gilgamesh will see you shortly." Babati left.

Shamhat waited, standing, as the sun moved and the shadows in the courtyard shifted position. The Wife of Gilgamesh's delay angered her. The temple needed her to help move things to higher ground in case the *Buranun* flooded. Her feet grew sore standing on the fire-baked brick floor. She and the Wife of Gilgamesh had once been friends. Now, despite her parched mouth and burning soles, she dared not presume to sit or take one of the gold beakers of beer sitting in a rack in the shade.

"Oh, Shamhat, you're finally here." The Wife of Gilgamesh strolled in, followed by two servants fanning her with ostrich feathers. She sat in her usual chair, picked up a beaker, and sipped. Shamhat's mouth watered.

"I haven't seen you at the temple lately," the Wife of Gilgamesh observed.

Shamhat took a breath to compose herself. "I've been busy with accounts and temple business. While I was away, work piled up."

"Temple accounts, yes. And rutting on the floor with the king's companion—does that count as temple business too?" The Wife of Gilgamesh snapped her fingers, and a servant rushed to her side with a gold platter piled high with dates and slices of pear.

Heat spread from Shamhat's chest to her neck and face. She fought the urge to look away. "I serve the Lady Inanna to the best of my abilities."

The Wife of Gilgamesh leaned forward, her eyes sharp in her plump face. "But you must serve the king, too. He has ordered me to tell you to 'not force your presence on Enkidu.'" A triumphant smile curved her lips.

Shamhat caught her breath. If she didn't see Enkidu, she'd have no way to influence the king, and Geshtu and Kirum would revolt. "As the king wishes." She arranged her features in a look of sympathy. "As you probably guessed with your great wisdom, I toyed with Enkidu for your sake."

"My sake?" The Wife of Gilgamesh popped a date in her mouth and studied Shamhat from under half-shut eyelids. "Why?"

"When I found Enkidu, he was running naked in the desert. He doesn't deserve to take your place in the king's affections." Shamhat added, as if in afterthought, "nor does he deserve to take your son's place as the logical heir."

The Wife of Gilgamesh blanched. "Out!" she ordered her servants.

Shamhat waited until she could no longer hear their sandals slap. "Inanna-Ama-Mu is no threat to you. He wishes only to be a priest. Enkidu, on the other hand. . ."

"Enkidu what?" The Wife of Gilgamesh leaned forward, gripping the abalone-inlaid arms of her chair.

"He swore he would defeat Gilgamesh. Right now, he may love the king and obey his every whim. But you are the daughter of a king and the wife of a king. You know ambition often wins out over love."

The Wife of Gilgamesh slumped. "The king no longer listens to my counsel. He never visits the children. He can't bear to be apart from his 'brother.' At night, they sleep in the same bed. When the king wants me, he calls me into his room and takes me with Enkidu there, watching." She gestured for Shamhat to sit on a bench.

She sank onto it gratefully. "May I open my liver to you?"

"You may."

"Since Enkidu arrived, the king no longer usurps the rights of bridegrooms or forces the young men into athletic contests. The people no longer fear him as if he were a wolf or lion."

"So my spies say."

"But Enkidu keeps Gilgamesh from his duties. The Eanna needs its walls repaired, and some city guards sleep on duty. Citizens have grievances the councilors can't solve. If I were to spend more time with Enkidu...."

The Wife of Gilgamesh sipped her beer. "You're suggesting I conspire against my husband and lord."

"In his own best interest. Besides, he ordered me not to pursue Enkidu. We wouldn't be breaking his command if sometimes you sent Enkidu to me."

"The king would be angry anyway. He mustn't find out." The Wife of Gilgamesh stood and adjusted her elaborately embroidered cloak. "I'll do it." Shamhat mouthed a brief prayer of thanks to Inanna. "But," the Wife of Gilgamesh warned, "if you trick or betray me, I will plunge a knife into Inanna-Ama-Mu's heart myself. No one will be heir but my Ur-Nungal."

Chapter 21: Poles and Poems

Uruk
Later that morning
Gilgamesh, Shamhat, Gilgamesh

CRACK! GILGAMESH PARRIED ENKIDU'S POPLAR STAFF at ankle height and jumped high. As he expected, Enkidu's staff whizzed beneath him. Gilgamesh flipped his stick up and whacked Enkidu on the head as he dropped, then took two quick steps backwards.

"Lord King, the fruit trees!" the gardener wailed. Gilgamesh barely had time to lift his staff before Enkidu swung again, this time at his waist. Gilgamesh parried, spun his staff to almost horizontal, and lunged forward, knocking Enkidu backwards and off balance. Now was his chance. He swung at Enkidu's knees, sure the blow would bring Enkidu down. Instead, Enkidu, wobbling, bent his knees and took the blow on his thigh. When Gilgamesh's staff hit home, Enkidu merely grunted. Gilgamesh's staff cracked.

Gilgamesh dropped the broken staff and darted for a replacement, knowing Enkidu would be right behind him. He grabbed a new staff and kept running, curving left around some quince trees. Enkidu must not have expected the move. He stopped, confused. Gilgamesh dashed toward him, angling his staff so it would connect with Enkidu's head.

Any other man would have raised his staff to face level. But Enkidu usually chose an offensive move over a defensive one. As Gilgamesh swung his staff at Enkidu's unprotected head, Enkidu lowered his staff and thrust it forward, its end aimed at Gilgamesh's stomach.

Gilgamesh twisted.

He was neither fast enough nor accurate enough. His staff merely ruffled Enkidu's hair, but Enkidu's staff caught him in the side, between rib and hipbone. Gilgamesh staggered forward, desperately struggling to maintain his balance. He would not lose to Enkidu. He would not. He had to be the better man.

But even his great will could not keep him on his feet. With a shout of rage, Gilgamesh fell to his knees. He had lost. He used his staff to help him stand, then in anger he broke it across his knee. He would have to concede.

But Enkidu was not standing in a victor's pose. He lay curled on the ground, his face twisted in agony.

Gilgamesh fell to his knees beside him. He took Enkidu's hand. "What's wrong?"

"My head. It hurts worse than before."

Gilgamesh squeezed his hand, and Enkidu winced. He looked down at Enkidu's hand. Enkidu's finger bulged on either side of the gold and lapis ring that had fit perfectly when Gilgamesh gave it to him. Gilgamesh placed Enkidu's hand down gently and stroked his hair. "I'll get you some poppy juice."

Enkidu grimaced. "It doesn't help anymore. Stay with me and sing. Sing one of Shamhat's praise poems."

The words hit him like one of Enkidu's staff blows. He had heard the priestesses sing Inanna's glory countless times, yet he had never wondered where the songs came from. They just *were*, as the *Buranun* just was, flowing day after day, with no beginning and no end. But in fact, Shamhat and the other priestesses wrote the poems.

Gilgamesh didn't know the words to any praise poem, so he hummed one. After a while, Enkidu's face relaxed, and his breathing became even.

Gilgamesh stopped humming and looked at his companion of the heart. He would be fine now. He had to be. The Gods would not let him be sick after sending him from the desert.

If Inanna, that cruel Goddess, deserved praise poems, then he, the greatest king in the world, surpassing all other men, did as well.

*   *   *

Loud singing, with an undercurrent of arguments and burping, issued from the door of Kirum's tavern. Priestesses were forbidden to enter taverns, so Shamhat went to the kitchen to wait.

She didn't wait long. Kirum rushed out from the tavern and headed toward the pigpen, huffing and carrying an armful of bowls. She jumped when Shamhat stepped forward. Shamhat reached out to steady the crockery. "*Ashe*! You startled me." Kirum set the bowls down.

"I didn't know where else to go. The king's given me another difficult task, perhaps more dangerous than the last."

"A task more dangerous than spending days in the desert with nomads and wild animals and taming a wild man? Bah!" Kirum took a spoon and scraped left-over lentils from the bowls into the pen. The pigs charged forward, snuffling and pushing. "You look tired. After a good night's sleep, you'll feel up to this new task."

"He wants me to write a praise poem."

"You do that often."

"A poem about him." Shamhat threw her hands up. "What do I praise about a king who has achieved so little? 'Great king Gilgamesh! Great is your disregard for your people! Great king Gilgamesh! Great is your appetite for virgins! Great king Gilgamesh! Great is your stomach for beer!'"

Kirum giggled. "For a priestess of Inanna, you don't know men very well. There's plenty you can say and fool him into thinking you've praised him."

"Such as what?"

"I listen to the men brag night after night. After a while, they all sound the same. Each claims *his* ancestors did the greatest deeds, *his* sheep have the finest wool, *his* wife is the hardest worker, *his* penis is the largest." A sow with swollen teats lumbered to the fence, and Kirum let it lick out the last bowl while she scratched it behind an ear. "After they're really drunk, they'll brag about how far away a target they can hit when they piss."

Laughing, Shamhat embraced Kirum. "You've saved me. Maybe I'll get back into the king's good graces." Shamhat returned to her room at the temple less agitated than she had been in months. Only one thing weighed on her mind. She put her hand on her belly. "Please, Great Queen of Heaven, let me not be carrying Enkidu's child."

On an evening four weeks later in Gilgamesh's bedroom, Babati bowed low. "Lord king, they're waiting for you in the garden—the high priests and priestesses of all the temples and shrines, your council of old men, your council of young men, and men of high rank."

Gilgamesh held up a copper mirror to check that the barber had trimmed his beard perfectly and braided strips of gold into his hair the way he had ordered. He wore a new fringed skirt of fine linen and jewel-studded sandals. "Is Shamhat there?"

"Yes. She waits on the dais."

"Have the lyre players precede me." He stood straight, with his chest out, his large cylinder seal of malachite topped with a gold bull visible for everyone to see. He picked up his staff of kingship with a ring-covered hand. The musicians began. He followed them in a stride that would highlight his vigor and height.

People packed the garden. The gardeners would be more annoyed than usual. But after hearing him praised like a God, they would be too awed to complain.

He stepped up on the dais of cedar wood, and the recently cut wood gave off a resinous, exotic scent. His head buzzed with excitement, and he frowned to keep from grinning like a boy.

"The priestess Shamhat, who serves Inanna, has written a new praise poem," he thundered. He sat on his gem-encrusted stool with his mother and wife on one side and Enkidu on the other.

Shamhat knelt before him, her back to the audience, her beautiful slanted eyes on him, eyes that had, unforgettably, looked into his in the Sacred Marriage bed. A musician from the temple sat behind her with a harp inlaid with carnelian and abalone and decorated with a bull's head carved from gold. Gilgamesh motioned for Shamhat to begin. The harpist plucked a melody, slapping the soundboard lightly at the ends of phrases. Then

Shamhat began. Her voice, strong and clear, was like the finest of beers.

"Who can doubt the greatness of Gilgamesh, king of Uruk?

"For his father was Lugalbanda the Pure, who wore the helmet called 'Lion of Battle,'

"For his father was Lugalbanda the Pure, who came alone from the mountains to lead the armies of King Enmerkar,

"For his father was Lugalbanda the Pure, who became a king and then a God.

"Who can doubt the greatness of Gilgamesh, king of Uruk?"

Gilgamesh nodded his head as the harpist played alone again. His father's reputation gilded his own.

"Who can doubt the greatness of Gilgamesh, king of Uruk?

"For his city, Uruk, is the greatest in the world,

"For his city, Uruk, was chosen by Inanna for Her house,

"For his city, Uruk, is fertile and filled with gardens,

"Who can doubt the greatness of Gilgamesh, king of Uruk?"

Gilgamesh frowned as the harpist played again. When was Shamhat going to get to *his* deeds, sing *his* praises? He looked at his wife. She smiled as if he truly were being praised, but *Ama* pursed her lips and drew her brows together.

"Who can doubt the greatness of Gilgamesh, king of Uruk?

"For his personal God, Utu, loves him more than all others,

"For his wife, the Wife of Gilgamesh, loves him more than all others,

"For his brother, Enkidu, loves him more than all others,

"Who can doubt the greatness of Gilgamesh, king of Uruk?"

The harpist played more and more slowly until she stopped, and then she backed away, bowing. Shamhat touched her head to the platform. Great Utu, she was done! Humiliation and anger brought heat to his face. He forced himself to smile, to stand, to retrieve from under the stool the gold earrings he no longer wanted to give her. "Rise, Shamhat, and approach."

With the grace of a gazelle, she swayed toward him, smiling.

"What are you doing?" he growled, keeping his voice low so no one would hear.

Her smile disappeared. "You requested a praise poem, great king."

"You played me for a fool in front of everyone important in Uruk. Where were the praises of my great deeds? My great projects? My generosity and fairness to my people?"

"What— Which— Which ones did you expect to hear of, my lord? I can add more verses." Her hands trembled at his displeasure, as well they should. If she had been anyone else, he would have cut her down. He glowered fiercely. "Truly, my lord, I can write more," she whispered, dropping her head. "What deeds should I add?"

He realized he had no answer.

Poets still sang of the many great deeds of Lugalbanda and how he rose from nothing to become a king. Unlike his father, Gilgamesh had done nothing worthy of even one poem of praise.

It was time to earn a reputation. He handed the earrings to Shamhat and before she could thank him, he turned, took Enkidu's hand, and led him to the front of the dais. "Hear me, my people. My brother, Enkidu, and I will go to the Cedar Forest, sacred to Enlil. We will kill the forest's guardian, Humbaba, and cut down the largest cedar tree."

The crowd erupted in angry shouts about his deserting them in the harvest and flood season, and his wife started crying. He ignored them all. If he killed Humbaba, what glory would be his! The name of Gilgamesh would live forever.

Chapter 22: Counsel Ignored

Uruk
The next morning
Shamhat, Enkidu

"QUEEN OF HEAVEN, WHAT HAVE I DONE?" Shamhat prostrated herself on the cold limestone floor before Inanna in Her cella. "A bad king is better than no king. Save Gilgamesh and Uruk from the wrath of Enlil."

"I didn't expect to find you here so early, but it saves me a trip to look for you." Nanna-Ur-Sag came in with a torch. "I will go to the king's great house today with the councils and *nin*-priestess Enlilla. I may need your services as a scribe."

"As you wish."

After the Goddess's first morning meal, Nanna-Ur-Sag and Shamhat took a boat and then walked to the great house into the public courtyard, already heated from the press of bodies and smelling of enough scented oils to give her a headache. Behind Gilgamesh stood Enkidu with an ostrich feather fan. Nanna-Ur-Sag excused his way to the front, and Shamhat followed in his wake.

As *en*-priest of the city's patron Goddess, Nanna-Ur-Sag spoke first. "Since the earliest times, the Cedar Forest has been sacred to Enlil and forbidden to humans. What you propose will anger Enlil. He already tried to wipe out humans once. Do you wish to be the cause of a second attempt? What will Inanna do if in the most dangerous time of the year you leave Her city leaderless?"

"Old man, you surprise me. The cold breath of Ereshkigal, Queen of the Netherworld, brushes your neck, as one day it will mine.

131

Humans die. Only deeds survive."

"Have you no care for Uruk?" Nanna-Ur-Sag asked. Gilgamesh turned toward the council of old men.

"Well, my advisors, what have you come to say to me?"

Nur-Ea stepped forward. "You are still young, lord king, and prone to whims. No one can kill Humbaba. We beg you, don't leave your city unguarded. Don't throw away your life in the prime of your manhood."

Gilgamesh barked a laugh. "Listen to them, Enkidu! They achieved no glory, so they begrudge me any." He turned his back on the council of old men, and they hissed when he looked toward the council of young men. "What do you have to say?"

A goldsmith friend of Geshtu's stepped forward. "Great king, some of us also yearn for glory. We want to go with you to the Cedar Forest. With the beat of drums as we march toward the forest, Humbaba will hear us coming and tremble! With the beat of drums as we march home, everyone will know of our great deed!"

Shamhat knew better. They wanted to avoid being conscripted to help with the harvest.

Gilgamesh nodded approvingly at the goldsmith, taking his words at face value. "You are brave, but this is not your time. For my name to live forever, I must do this alone. Nanna-Ur-Sag, you'll watch over the city in my stead. Let your scribe write the words, and I will add my mark."

Shamhat drew a line under her notes, drafted a hasty contract in the lower register, and took it to Gilgamesh. He rolled his cylinder seal across the clay.

Gilgamesh stood, and rustling filled the courtyard as everyone except the *en*-priest and *nin*-priestess bowed. He swaggered out of the courtyard, Enkidu following. The back of Shamhat's neck tingled. Gilgamesh leaving the city would invite disaster. She had to persuade Enkidu to change his mind.

"I don't want to go to the Cedar Forest," Enkidu pouted.

"You have to." Gilgamesh walked toward the forge. "Why are you scared?"

Enkidu fingered his lion teeth. "I've fought lions and wolves and panthers. They were puppies compared with Humbaba. He has the blessing of Enlil."

Gilgamesh laughed. "When did you become so pious? We all die. Come with me and your name will live forever."

"I don't care about glory. I just want to be with you."

Gilgamesh went into the forge. Enkidu waited outside. It was hotter than the hottest day in the desert in the forge, and he hated the noise the smiths made beating their hammers. It always triggered one of his headaches. They came more and more often now, and his head felt too heavy to hold up.

Something jostled his elbow. He looked down. "Shamhat!"

"Come visit me tonight in the garden of scents in Inanna's house." She slipped away as soon as he agreed. The minutes passed quickly as he daydreamed about the pleasures of the night to come.

Gilgamesh stomped out of the forge, his face lit with joy. "The smiths are already busy at work. Each of our axes will weigh more than two Nanna-Ur-Sags. Our knives will have oak handles and gold-plated quillons. My helmet will be decorated with a gold lion's head and yours with a silver aurochs' head." He took Enkidu's hand. "Let's go to the shrine of Ninsun to get my mother's blessing."

At the shrine, priestesses bowed as Gilgamesh led Enkidu to his mother's room. She sat on her pallet, sewing. She looked up at their entrance and her face fell. "Are you here to say goodbye?"

Her sadness hurt Enkidu's chest. He sat beside her and held her hand.

"What a good boy you are, Enkidu. But you can't protect me from sorrow."

"*Ama*, I've come to ask your blessing," Gilgamesh said, pacing. "We will face the fierce Humbaba, whom no one has defeated."

She went to a chest and took out a jeweled necklace and a colored belt, which she put on. She splashed water on her face from a basin of reeds coated in pitch. "Let's go to the courtyard. I will pray to your patron, Utu."

In the courtyard, the priestess lit pine chips in a copper bowl. It smelled sweet and reminded Enkidu of Shamhat. The priestess lifted up her arms to the sun. "Great Utu, Who lights the world, wakes all creatures, and fills people with the joy of day, You have given my son so many gifts. Why have You burdened him with a restless *zi*? Because of You, he will make a dangerous trip to Enlil's forest. While You shine, protect him and keep his legs strong on his long journey. When he faces Humbaba, make the winds blow, and send a great storm to make it easier for my son to kill him. Lord Utu, protect him and bring him home to his mother."

She turned to Enkidu and transferred her jeweled necklace from her neck to his. "My dear Enkidu, you have been a brother to Gilgamesh. Although you did not come from my womb, I claim you as my son. I'll have a contract made, and I'll roll my seal on it."

Enkidu's eyes grew hot and wet with tears. They poured down his face and dampened his beard. "*Ama*," he said. "*Ama*." He once sobbed the same words next to a woman's lion-ravaged corpse. He had grown much bigger since then. Now he could protect his family. "*Ama*, don't be sad about Gilgamesh. I will teach him the ways of the desert and protect him."

"I know you will, dear one." She smiled at him sweetly. "The Gods meant you to stand by his side."

Gilgamesh's *side*. They were brothers. Equals. Yet Gilgamesh was always head male. For the first time, Enkidu wondered when his own turn would come.

Chapter 23: So Soon to Leave

Uruk
That afternoon
Shamhat

SHAMHAT FINISHED A TABLET AND TOOK IT OUTSIDE to dry. She usually worked in the scribe room later than this, but she wanted to visit the temple bathhouse before Enkidu's visit.

As she headed toward the bathhouse, a first-year girl ran toward her, crying out, "A man is waiting for you at the gate!"

"Thank you, little sister. But remember, we do not shout or run in Inanna's house." The girl hung her head. Shamhat turned and headed toward the gate, wishing she'd been more specific in telling Enkidu what time to come.

But at the gate she found not Enkidu, but Dabta. He panted as he leaned against the building. "Lady Shamhat, Nameshda is very sick. Your brother says to come quickly."

Something squeezed inside her chest. "Rest here, and then tell the *en*-priest where I've gone. I'll go on ahead."

When she got to the house, Nameshda lay in the courtyard in a new bed. To the left of the bed stood an empty chair, and beside it sat flat bread and beer for Nameshda's *zi* to consume after death. To the right of the bed, *Ama* twisted her gnarled hands together. Shamhat sagged, then forced herself to Nameshda's side. Shamhat put her ear to Nameshda's nose and chest. She breathed, but shallowly, and beads of sweat dotted her skin. Geshtu gestured to her from the corner, where he stood with Kirum. Their eyes were rimmed with red.

"I will offer a statuette to Inanna on her behalf," Shamhat said.

135

"No, it's too late." Geshtu snuffled, then continued in the tone he used when doing business with his customers. "Kirum needs to know how many mourners I want to rent."

"The cost varies." Kirum consulted her tablet. "Prostitutes are cheaper than professional mourners, but the professionals never cause trouble. I can also hire some lyre players. Do you know whether Nameshda had a personal God? Or do you know what priest you want?"

Shamhat rubbed her tight forehead. "Our family will look mean-spirited if we hire few mourners. On the other hand, will Gilgamesh take offense if we mourn Nameshda too bold? After all, she dies by the king's hand."

"By the king's 'staff,' you mean." Anger sparked in Geshtu's eyes. "There's also Nur-Ea to consider. If we shortchange his daughter, will he renege on his promise to put me on the council of young men?"

Kirum consulted her tablet again. "You'll need a coffin and some men to dig up the floor above your crypt. Would you like me to take care of those arrangements?"

"There's a friend's discount, I assume?" Geshtu asked bluntly. When Kirum agreed, he said, "Twelve professional mourners, a cedar coffin, six men to dig, any priest." Kirum hugged Shamhat and left.

"Would you like me to choose clothes and jewelry for the burial?" Shamhat asked. Geshtu nodded, remaining in the corner, the skin of his face slack. Shamhat hugged him. "You shouldn't punish your wife by denying her the comfort of your presence."

"She wouldn't want me there." His voice was bitter. "It was my responsibility to protect her, and I didn't."

"It doesn't matter now. Pray beside her and hold her hand so her *zi* goes easily when her Gods invite her."

Over the next week, Shamhat and *Ama* took turns caring for Nameshda, with Kirum lending a hand when she could. One day, when death seemed close, Shamhat went to buy some scented oil. By the time she got back, Nameshda had returned to the clay, harvested by the Gods while in the fields humans harvested crops.

Burly laborers were already digging up the indoor courtyard floor. Geshtu wandered from room to room in his ripped clothes, holding a brass lamp and trailing an embroidered sash behind him. "What grave goods should I send with her? Whom should I invite? Do you remember whether I need to tip the laborers? What gifts should we give the mourners?"

Shamhat took the lamp and sash from him. "Rest now," she said. "*Ama* and I will prepare the body. Then I'll help you get everything ready for the mourners tomorrow." She followed him to his bedroom. "We did this together for *Ada*. We can do it for Nameshda."

She went into *Ama*'s room, to the bed and chest *Ama* kept there for her, and took off all her jewelry and hair ornaments. She placed them in the chest along with her sandals. She took off her fine linen shawl and found one of undyed wool. She ripped it in several places and put it on.

Dabta ushered Nur-Ea into the courtyard as Shamhat left her mother's room. "My daughter lies here unattended? For shame!" Nur-Ea blustered. "And double shame that these are all the grave goods you provide for her."

"Lord Nur-Ea, this is a house of mourning." Shamhat could barely hear herself speak. Although she'd never known Nameshda, she still felt as if her breath had been knocked out of her. "We have barely begun preparations for Nameshda's burial. Please honor her with your quiet."

He dismissed her request with a curt motion of his hand. He looked about, his mouth twisted. "Where is Geshtu? My daughter died childless, so he must return her dowry."

Shamhat dared to look at him in reproving silence. Nur-Ea at last dropped his gaze and went to a bench along the wall. He sat and put his face in his hands, and his shoulders shook. Shamhat narrowed her eyes. If Nur-Ea and the rest of the council of old men had acted to rein in Gilgamesh, Nameshda would still be alive.

Shamhat motioned to Dabta. "Please help me carry her into the kitchen." They placed her gently on the table. "That's all, Dabta." *Ama* had already begun preparations. Buckets of water sat next to the table, and a folded clean shawl lay on a bench, along with the oil Shamhat had bought at the market. Only *Ama* wasn't ready. She sat on the bench, folded and slumped into a person half her usual size, her arms around herself.

Shamhat began alone. She undressed the body and set aside the clothes, which stank of fever and sickness, for burning. She picked up a folded piece of linen, dipped it in a barrel, and gently washed Nameshda's face and neck. She looked a worn-out, withered thirty, not a fresh, plump thirteen. Shamhat took a long strip of cloth, wrapped it under Nameshda's jaw, and tied the ends tightly on top of her head. She wrung out the linen, dipped it into the barrel again, and started on a shoulder. *Ama* heaved herself from the bench and came to help.

Ama sang the ritual song of washing the dead, and Shamhat joined in. They said not a word to each other, but when they reached the abdomen, *Ama* placed Shamhat's hand on the bulge on Nameshda's belly, made more obvious by her now-bony frame. Shamhat closed her eyes. Geshtu didn't know, and she wouldn't tell him. No need to fuel his already ferocious anger at the king.

But the similar bulge on Shamhat's belly could not remain a secret much longer.

Although Shamhat had sent Dabta to deliver news of Nameshda's death, the funeral was sparsely attended. Most of the city had lined up early to watch Gilgamesh leave on his quest, several guests quietly told her.

Shamhat stared into the dark burial pit at the crypt as the gravediggers lowered Nameshda's body. Here she stood again, so soon. The cold scent of earth and decay wafted up, and the professional mourners wailed more loudly. *Ama* sniffled, and Geshtu kept clearing his throat. Shamhat raked her fingernails down her cheeks, mourning both Nameshda and herself. She welcomed the tingle and pain, relief from her grief, and she scratched again. Her fingernails came away bloody.

She had thought taming Enkidu was Inanna's will. She had used wool soaked in pomegranate juice as an extra precaution. Yet the Goddess had allowed her to grow with child.

Nameshda's body now lay in the crypt with *Ada* and his ancestors. The workers lowered the grave goods—several *kulis* of beer, a basket of fruits, a basket of breads, several shawls, silver jewelry, cosmetics, scented oil, Nameshda's cylinder seal. There was nothing for the child within Nameshda but one thing: Shamhat had hidden a small clay doll at the bottom of the bread basket.

She would have to tell Nanna-Ur-Sag about her pregnancy and accept his punishment. But she would wait. It was still early; many children were invited to the Gods before ever taking a breath.

The gravediggers climbed out of the pit and pulled the ladder up. The men began shoveling the dirt they had removed yesterday into the pit. Shamhat took one last look at the tomb where *Ada* and Nameshda lay and then backed out of the way of the workmen.

It was too familiar. She couldn't breathe. The heat of the bodies pressed tightly together, the smell of garlic in such a close space, the thuds and slithers as the dirt hit the crypt and slid off overwhelmed her. Despite the priest's frown, she rushed toward the street and fresh air.

She turned at a hand on her shoulder. Geshtu's face, bleak and vacant, had new lines she suspected would never go away. "I felt as if I were at *Ada*'s funeral again," he mumbled.

"Me too." Shamhat and Geshtu leaned against each other, propping each other up. The crowd waiting for the king stood eerily silent. The beating of drums rumbled in Shamhat's chest, their rhythm at odds with the pounding of her heart.

Geshtu roused from his stupor. "What's happening? This is no feast day."

"The king's leaving. He wants to do a 'great deed' so his reputation will live forever."

Color and expression returned to Geshtu's face. He shoved his way through the crowds, ignoring curses, and Shamhat followed. They reached the street as the jugglers passed by. After the jugglers came beautiful women playing lyres and then cages of lions, seven rows three abreast. No one cheered. At last the king and Enkidu appeared on litters covered in gold leaf, each carried by eight men.

The crowd at last responded. "Don't leave us during flood season!" a woman cried in a raw, broken voice. Seven men burst from the crowd and threw themselves on the ground in front of the litters. The bearers stopped, and Gilgamesh, frowning, pushed himself into a seated position.

He glared at the crowd, then focused on the woman who had shouted first. "I go to win glory for Uruk as well as myself."

"The shepherd shouldn't leave the sheepfold unguarded." A cheer exploded.

Gilgamesh turned red with anger. "I'm a king and should do kingly deeds!"

The woman did not back down. "You should care for Uruk the Sheepfold. We deserve someone who'll repair the temples and canals and roads, who'll judge and punish the guilty, who'll help the widows and orphans." The crowd cheered her again.

Scowling, Gilgamesh gestured his bearers forward. Shamhat held her breath, but the bearers stepped around the men in the road.

As they passed, Enkidu turned his head and looked right at her. Shamhat at last remembered she had planned to see him and ask him to turn Gilgamesh from this quest. Caring for Nameshda had put their meeting completely out of her mind. Now Enkidu left, looking as confused as the first time she offered him bread. She put her hand on her belly and offered a prayer to Inanna to protect Enkidu and Uruk from Gilgamesh's folly.

Two weeks later, Shamhat's face still bore the marks of her mourning. "The scabs on your cheeks look as if they'll leave scars. You should have mourned with more restraint. You represent Inanna to the people." Nanna-Ur-Sag was always irritable nowadays. He was more harried than ever, thanks to Gilgamesh putting him in charge of the city. He shuffled through tablets on the archive shelves, squinting at each in the dim light provided by an oil lamp as he searched for the contracts the council of old men had asked to see.

Shamhat turned her face away. "Nameshda was part of my family, and her death was another affront to Inanna by Gilgamesh."

Nanna-Ur-Sag's face twisted with worry. "My dream must have been false. Enkidu has not humbled the king." He glanced at her belly, then away. He hadn't asked her yet, and Shamhat hadn't told him. "You've paid a heavy price for my wrong dream, and now we must find a way to appease the Gods."

"Nur-Ea told my brother you attend all the council meetings and make sensible decisions. Perhaps the council of old men will elect you king."

Nanna-Ur-Sag huffed a laugh. "Kings collect cities like women collect jewelry. If an old priest like me took the throne today, tomorrow the kings of Ur, Eridu, and Larsa would be camped outside our gates. No, my daughter, the king's main duties may be administrative, but nonetheless he must be a warrior."

A *kurgarra* ran into the library. "The river!" he gasped, then sneezed several times from the pulverized clay dust. Shamhat's thoughts flew to Geshtu's house, which sat near a canal.

"Is the *Buranun* rising?" Nanna-Ur-Sag asked tensely.

"Worse. The city is under attack. Outside the north river gate."

Nanna-Ur-Sag shoved the tablets in his hands onto the nearest empty shelf. "Shamhat, go to your friend the tavernkeeper. Tell the customers to arm themselves and go to the north gate." He followed the *kurgarra* as fast as his elderly legs could take him.

Shamhat made no pretense of dignity as she ran, her shawl flapping and the wind pulling her hair free of her headdress. She ran in the forbidden door of the tavern, and Kirum dropped a beaker of beer in her surprise. Curious, Shamhat glanced around. Men sat in clusters around tall jars of beer, drinking through straws. Several leered at her, and one called an invitation to sit on his lap. The prostitutes sneered.

"The city's north gate is under attack." She had to raise her voice to be heard. "Inanna's *en*-priest orders you all to arm yourselves and go to the north gate. Tell everyone you meet to do the same." Men scraped back their stools and benches and stood, dumping prostitutes on the floor. Some left the tavern at a run, but others hung back.

"I'm a carpenter. I know nothing of fighting."

"I have a game leg."

"Well, don't just stand there." Kirum slammed down a *kuli*. "If you won't fight, tell the smiths and the physicians what's happening. They'll be needed." The men left, and Kirum let down the mat over the tavern door. "What does Nanna-Ur-Sag want the women to do?"

"He didn't say." Shamhat's gaze fell on an abandoned beaker, now lying on its side spilling beer onto the dirt floor. "The men will need beer. And food. What else? Sheets to clean and wrap wounds."

"Those who don't fight should go somewhere safe."

"The Eanna. It has the tallest wall in town." Shamhat sucked in her breath. "Inanna-Ama-Mu is at the temple of An. I must get him!"

Kirum shook Shamhat. "He's as safe there as at the Eanna. We have to think about *all* the children."

"You're right." Shamhat sighed. "Besides, how would I explain why I came for him?"

Kirum shook her again. "How shall we do this?"

"I'll ask the temple staff to round up women, children, and old people. Go to the other tavernkeepers. Ask them to send donkeys with beer to the north gate. Ask the bakers to send bread."

They split up. Shamhat ran to her brother's house to tell him about the attack and to ask Dabta to take *Ama* to the Eanna. She ran to the temple and raced through it, urging priestesses, slaves, and free workers to bring people to the temple. The cooks and bakers began working at double speed to prepare for the influx.

Shamhat made countless trips. When the sky filled with smoke and a horrible stench reached the Eanna, several children panicked and tried to run out into the street to go home. Nanna-Ur-Sag's second-in-command ordered all the gates bolted and guards posted. Shamhat herded a group of mothers and children into an empty storage room and sank to the brick floor in exhaustion.

The smallest children began to cry, and those without mothers clawed at Shamhat's skin as they climbed onto her. They were safe for now, and yet Shamhat shook in terror, for herself and for her children. It had been far easier facing the bull aurochs in the desert. She could see her enemy then. Now, anything could be happening.

She feared many city men would not have the faintest idea what to do in battle. The butchers could swing their cleavers, and the shoemakers, their awls. But most of the defenders would have only stone knives. What if an army with weapons of bronze attacked their gates? She wished Zaidu were here, solid and calm and brave.

The older children started crying next, as well as some of the women. Shamhat offered empty words of comfort as they sat and waited. Women always sat and waited while their men went off. Even the Wife of Gilgamesh had to sit and wait for her foolish husband like the poorest of the poor.

They waited for hours. Shamhat prayed much of the time. Twice, she sent the calmest women to fetch bread and beer. A cook helped them bring it back. Each time, he had no news about the attack. As they passed out the food, the storehouse became quieter. The smallest children got sleepy after drinking their beer and dozed on their mothers' laps.

What was Inanna-Ama-Mu doing now? Was he scared or brave? Was he taking care of the younger priests-in-training? Was Kirum safe?

Was Geshtu still alive?

When twilight came, the older children curled up on the brick floor. Shamhat left the storeroom. The smoke in the courtyard made her cough. To the north, the sky flamed orange. Fire. The reed huts in the poor districts would burn quickly. As she watched, cold with terror, the orange didn't spread. Perhaps the men of Uruk had the enemy in their grasp.

Perhaps this. Perhaps that. She would have preferred to be at the gates with a spear in her hand, like Inanna. The Goddess ignored the usual boundaries of male and female and gloried in war. Perhaps She fought alongside the men at this very moment wearing Her horned headdress. Perhaps She let them fight alone in Her anger at Gilgamesh.

Perhaps, perhaps. Shamhat waited and worried, the lot of women.

Chapter 24: Spoils of War

Uruk
The next morning
Shamhat

"THE *EN*-PRIEST IS BACK!" The joyous shout woke Shamhat. After a glance at the sleeping children, she straightened her shawl and ran outside. Priestesses threw open the front gate, and Nanna-Ur-Sag limped in. In a moment, he was surrounded by the staff and priestesses, Shamhat among them. Though filthy and hollow-eyed, he was smiling and leading by a rope several sullen, sooty men with their hands tied behind their backs.

"Is the city safe?" Shamhat asked. Smoke still hung heavy.

"Are you injured?" asked a priestess.

"Who attacked us?" asked another.

Nanna-Ur-Sag threw up his hands. "I need a bath and some food. Put the new slaves with the others. But yes, Uruk is safe."

Shamhat returned to the storeroom and woke the refugees. "It's safe to go home." The temple grounds became chaotic as mothers separated from their children ran about and shouted their names.

Shamhat looked at the sun. Inanna needed her first morning meal, but many of the male staff had gone to fight, and the other priestesses had their hands full. She went to the kitchen. Inanna's meal waited. Shamhat balanced a tray of bread on her head and a jug of beer on her hip and took them herself to the cella. No torches lit the room, and the remains of the previous day's meals still remained. She shoved them aside to make room for the bread she had brought. She could not empty the alabaster libation vase—it weighed six times as much as she did—so she poured the new beer in with the old. She stood before Inanna and sang some of the praise songs she had composed.

When she finished, she was reluctant to leave. She missed the rituals, the holy ambience and scent of smoke and oil in the cella, the rows of wide-eyed statuettes with their hands clasped in prayer, and the fearsome beauty of Inanna Herself. She knelt and thanked Inanna for saving the city.

She went out into the noise and bustle of the rest of the Eanna and joined the people clustered around Nanna-Ur-Sag. "Our attackers were three bands of nomads that joined together when they heard Uruk had no king. We greatly outnumbered them, but they knew how to fight, and most of our men didn't. We lost many men—"

Shamhat's stomach clenched, wondering whether Geshtu was among them. He was no fighter, preferring quieter pursuits such as carving and playing board games.

When her mind snapped back to what Nanna-Ur-Sag was saying, he was listing the damages. "Every tannery was destroyed, and several tanner families died. There'll be no new leather for some time. Part of the wharf burned. That will limit how many traders can dock. We lost a field of sesame. About two sixties of men died, and triple that many have injuries."

"*Meliea!*" a young priestess said. "Now everyone will think us easy game and attack."

The *en*-priest looked embarrassed. "The council of old men has granted me more powers as acting regent. I have stationed men on top of the walls around the city to watch for attack. I conscripted two hundred of the men who fought best to be a standing army."

"What's that?" a weaver interrupted.

"They'll leave their trades to be soldiers. They'll train every day and always be ready to fight." He glanced down at the length of his shadow. "There are temple duties to attend to now."

Shamhat headed for the gate. She had to make sure her family and Kirum were safe. Other citizens had the same idea. It was even more crowded outside the temple grounds than within. People scurried every which way, some purposelessly, some checking in at each shop and home. The men who had fought trudged home, and physicians urged slaves carrying litters of the injured to hurry. Every boat on the canals was filled.

It took much longer than usual to get home—to get to Geshtu's house, rather—and her heart was in her throat by the time she arrived. She found Dabta in the kitchen cooking barley and *Ama* and Geshtu in the interior courtyard. *Ama* had been through many trials in her years; although her face sagged with fatigue, she sat and spun as if this day were any other.

Geshtu sprawled in a chair staring at nothing, his hair tangled and his skirt and skin stained. He smelled of smoke and sweat and blood. "Get me some beer," he croaked.

Shamhat brought him a beer, as well as several wet cloths and a jar of oil. As he drank, she cleaned his face and then knelt and took off his sandals to wash his feet.

"I killed the king yesterday," he said conversationally. Shamhat cried out, then realized it couldn't be true. "I killed him over and over, and then I kicked his dead bodies."

"Are you avenged?" Shamhat's voice shook.

"No." He rubbed his eyes. "No matter how many times I killed, it didn't help. The stain on my honor runs too deep. No amount of blood can wash it away."

She shuddered at his strange words. "Please, I beg you, give up your vendetta against the king."

A single tear ran down Geshtu's face. "Revenge is bitter and unfulfilling."

Shamhat sobbed with joy as she rubbed oil onto his feet, her shoulders now free of one burden.

Two months later, as Shamhat worked on accounts in the scribes' room, she heard a familiar voice. "Shamhat! Thank all the Gods I found you."

Shamhat looked up. "Geshtu? I thought you'd be training now." Geshtu hadn't been chosen for the standing army, but like many men, he had volunteered to train part time.

"Come with me." He led her through streets of panicked citizens. Many streamed into the temples and shrines. Entire families, bent over from the weight of their belongings piled on their backs, abandoned their homes. Their feet churned the dry road dust, and Shamhat covered her nose with the edge of her shawl. The street rang with noise, and Geshtu could not hear her shouted questions.

They left the city by the north gate and walked onto the crowded, partially repaired wharves. She looked at the *Buranun* as everyone else was doing. On its surface bobbed a long, dark object, which she mistook at first for a marsh crocodile. But it was longer and more evenly shaped than any crocodile. Men waded toward it, nets and hooks in hands.

"The king has done it now." Geshtu stood with his arms folded, his body in his new soldier's stance, his voice hostile. "The Gods cannot ignore this sin."

"I don't understand. What's he done?"

He pointed to several other long, dark objects piled on the riverbank. Logs! She went closer and took a sniff. Cedar.

Geshtu had followed her. "There's more coming." He pointed upstream. The further up the river she looked, the denser the logs, until in the distance the *Buranun* seemed to flow with wood, not water.

"He didn't cut down one holy tree." It hurt to speak, her throat was so tight. "He cut down the whole sacred forest." An incredible sacrilege, one she could hardly believe even Gilgamesh would be arrogant enough to commit. No wonder the citizens panicked. Enlil's sacred place had been destroyed; the bad-tempered God would surely take revenge. "I have to return to the temple to pray that the Gods spare us."

"I'll stay here. After the nomad attack, I think many will be eager to rise against the king."

"No! You said you'd abandoned revenge."

Geshtu crossed his arms. "I said nothing about punishment."

Chapter 25: Insurrection

Uruk
Late that afternoon
Gilgamesh

A S ENKIDU STEERED THE RAFT of cedar logs lashed together, Gilgamesh cradled Humbaba's head on his lap, even though it now stank badly. The forest of logs floating ahead of them should be evidence enough of his great deed. But Humbaba's ugly visage—uglier now that the flesh had blanched and started to cave in—would prove he had defeated Enlil's champion.

"No one can doubt now I'm the greatest man in the world. Now there'll be songs about my deeds." Gilgamesh yawned. "Yours too, Enkidu," he added as an afterthought.

"I hope for a party with lots of beer," Enkidu said wistfully, rubbing his head as if it pained him again. Gilgamesh chuckled. Enkidu still lived in the moment like the near-animal he once was. He had no concept of history or of his name living on.

"Certainly there'll be a party in our honor. There's a fortune in timber floating toward Uruk. I can spruce up my great house and every temple and shrine. Cedar will burn day and night. My people will welcome us with dancing and singing and beer of every color and kind."

"Beer. Good."

Gilgamesh daydreamed as they rode the *Buranun* south. His citizens would look at him with awe and cheer him. Shamhat would compose another praise poem, this time praising *him*. He would find another heroic deed for the two of them to do.

Soon, the coppery walls of Uruk beckoned. He could see the dock workers capturing the logs and pulling them to the banks. People awaited him on the dock. But when they floated closer, he realized much of the dock was gone, burned to charred stubs, and scorch marks marred the city wall. The welcoming committee didn't look very welcoming. There were no musicians, no dancers, no women, just men standing rigid and unsmiling.

Men he recognized as his own citizens. Some he had called "friend."

Gilgamesh leaned forward, squinting. "What do you make of that?"

Enkidu huffed with annoyance. "No beer after all. We fight."

How dare they ruin his triumphant moment with a rebellion? They were among the luckiest men in the world, to live in Uruk. Gilgamesh set Humbaba's head down and reached for Enkidu's armor. He strapped it on Enkidu and then set the aurochs' head helmet on his head. Then he armed himself. He set Enkidu's battle axe at his feet and took up his own, standing with the axe raised above him as the raft skirted the wall and edged toward the wharf.

Three twelves of men against two. Not bad odds, except the waiting men had bows. Gilgamesh assessed their weapons and their faces. Close combat gave the best odds. Then Gilgamesh's and Enkidu's longer arms would give them an edge, and arrows would be worthless except for stabbing.

An arrow plunked against Gilgamesh's armor and bounced off, leaving a ding. Enkidu roared with anger. Gilgamesh picked up the arrow and rummaged through their equipment for bows. His spirits soared at the thought of a new battle. He shook his axe at the waiting men, taunting them to waste more arrows. A barrage flew. Many landed in the water, while others clattered harmlessly onto the raft. Lugal-Ki-Ag dropped his bow and ran back inside the city, apparently losing his nerve.

"I protect you," Enkidu said.

"What fun is that?" Gilgamesh tipped his head and laughed. "I say we wager on who can kill the most men."

"I have nothing to wager except my lion skin. Everything else I have you gave me."

"Wager your lion skin for . . . let's say, a day as king. You can do anything you want as if you were the greatest in the land."

Enkidu shot him a look Gilgamesh couldn't interpret. "Yes." He used a pole to keep the raft from bumping into the city wall. The men on the burned wharf crowded together, too close for good fighting, their faces grim. The archers shot more frequently and more accurately now. Gilgamesh picked up a bow and several arrows and shot. Men toppled.

Under his breath, Gilgamesh said, "Don't wait for the raft to bump the wharf. Let's jump a moment before and catch them off guard."

The men broke ranks when Gilgamesh and Enkidu leaped forward, roaring. Before the rebels could regroup, Gilgamesh and Enkidu barrelled into them, knocking several over. Enkidu picked up one and threw him against the city wall to smash like a spoiled cucumber. He tossed another far into the river. Enkidu was two for Gilgamesh's none. Gilgamesh spun once, twice, thrice, his battle axe cutting a swath around him, blood spraying and bodies piling around his turning feet. Several more men ran away, but five ran to the edge of the dock, turned, and aimed their arrows in unison.

Gilgamesh dropped to his knees, picked up a large body, and used it as a shield. He dropped his battle axe and seized two spears from the fallen. He aimed for the helmeted man who seemed to be giving orders and who had the most confident pose. Since when did his citizens wear helmets? The man saw his intention and opened his mouth to shout. Gilgamesh's spear went through his throat, and the man dropped his gear and, gurgling, scrabbled frantically at his neck.

The other archers shot carelessly, one at Gilgamesh and three at Enkidu. But the rebels had not factored in Enkidu's years among the gazelles. He jumped high, clearing the arrows, and landed in front of the archers. An arrow tore through the skin of Gilgamesh's upper arm. Roaring, he ripped it out as several men jumped onto him from behind and bore him down. The boards of the wharf stank of fire, fresh blood, and old fish.

"You! Get his helmet off!" one of his attackers ordered. "You and you, slice through the back of his heels."

Lame was a good as dead for a warrior–king. Gilgamesh kicked like a donkey and held onto his helmet with his one free hand. The weight of another body landed on him, and then another, and another. They would not have to lay a finger on him. He could not draw breath under their combined weight. The edges of his vision darkened.

Enkidu's roar pierced the air, and the man tugging at the straps of Gilgamesh's helmet abruptly stopped. More screams, followed by thuds and splashes. He could breathe again! He sucked in the air as his anger rose. He threw himself up with a growl, men still clinging to him. He shook himself like a wet dog, flinging off attackers.

Gilgamesh grabbed two traitors by their necks and crashed their heads together. The skulls smashed like soft-boiled eggs, and brains oozed out. He screamed with blood lust. A knife slashed and caught him across the knee. Again, a flesh wound, but it made him angrier. "Utu!" he cried out, and was rewarded with strength beyond any he had ever known. He looked for his battle axe among the bodies, casually backhanding a man who lunged at him with a knife. The man landed stunned at the edge of the dock. His head fell off and splashed into the river, courtesy of Enkidu's battle axe, leaving a neck stump spurting blood. Men screamed.

"Out of my way!" Gilgamesh shouted at Enkidu. He was immune to harm at this moment, safe under the protection of Utu. He felt the stabs of arrows and spears as mere pinpricks. Again he spun. Again, he cut down every man in his path. Breathing more roughly than usual, he stopped and looked for more victims.

Enkidu held his side, puffing hard. "Time for beer?"

"As soon as we count the dead."

Enkidu couldn't count. With a halting gait, he collected weapons from the corpses and pointed out his kills. "Did I win?"

"We came out even." Gilgamesh grimaced at not winning, then said reluctantly, "You can be king for a day, and I get your lion skin." Gilgamesh jumped onto the raft and picked up Humbaba's head by the hair. As his excitement wore off, his thoughts turned to revenge. He would punish the families of those who lay dead on the dock.

The ones who ran away, he would put to death.

* * *

Gilgamesh had never seen the streets of Uruk so empty. A sheep wandered free, bleating its distress and following some pigs. Untied gates banged. Each house they passed was like a tomb. No one worked outside or sang inside. The air held no perfume of onions or meat. On one roof, some laundry draped over reed racks dried. A breeze lifted a sheet and dropped it in the street. No one came after it.

"I left the *en*-priest in charge. Let's go to the Eanna."

"Beer first." Enkidu pointed to a tavern. He had been breathing hard since the fight, so Gilgamesh agreed. The tavern was empty, as every other building they had looked in had been. But a huge jar nearly full of *kashsi* sat on a stool. Each grabbed several straws, and they made short work of the beer. Gilgamesh's anger softened, and Enkidu breathed more easily.

Gilgamesh rummaged about until he found a fresh tablet the owner had been using to run tabs. He set it next to the beer jar and ran his cylinder seal across it and set a ring of silver next to it. "It's important to always pay your beer tab, Enkidu. Remember that."

Arms around each other's shoulders—Enkidu now stood taller than Gilgamesh—they lurched toward the Eanna. The wooden gates were barred from the inside when they got there. Gilgamesh banged several times, but no one answered. His mood got hot again. How dare they bar the temple to the king? "You run at the left gate, and I'll run at the right. Let's see who gets in first."

Enkidu ran without waiting for a signal and crashed against the gate like a mad aurochs. Wood cracked and echoed in the empty streets as the gate posts shuddered. Gilgamesh ran at the right gate, turning sidewards so his shoulder and hip hit. Enkidu ran at his gate again without any strategy, then sank to the ground. Gilgamesh studied his gate, then aimed several good kicks. The gate fell into the Eanna, pulling the door post with it. Frightened cattle bawled and ran, kicking up dust.

Gilgamesh dashed through and grabbed the arm of the first person he saw. "The *en*-priest. Where is he?" The frightened girl pointed toward the building that held the cella. "You'll have to wait, lord king. The Goddess is having her first evening meal."

He tightened his grip until she squealed. "Never tell a king what to do. Next time I won't be so generous." He flung her away, and she sprawled in the dirt. Fear and tears filled her eyes. He stomped past, calling for Enkidu, and headed for the cella. "Priest!" he shouted. "What madness have you allowed in my city?"

Servants and guards tried to block his way. He shoved them aside, following the sound of singing, getting angrier by the moment. When he was a few feet from the doorway, Shamhat came running from the other direction, her bewitching eyes wide with surprise. Her gait lurched, and a look at her belly showed why.

"Harlot!" he snarled at her. "You have dishonored the temple of the city's patron. You will bring down Inanna's wrath."

She draped a protective arm across her belly and glanced at Enkidu. Then she looked at Gilgamesh, her eyes seething. "At your order, lord king. I tamed the wild man at *your* order."

Gilgamesh would deal with her insolence later. He turned to enter the cella, but Shamhat continued, shouting. "My shame and dishonor are nothing compared with yours! Every bride fears and hates you. Your citizens hide from you. You dishonor the temples by letting them fall into disrepair. Instead of doing your duties, you and Enkidu play like overgrown children."

"Quiet, woman!" Gilgamesh bellowed. "It's your duty to sacrifice for your king!"

The *en*-priest slipped out the doorway of the cella. "Please, I beg you, be quiet during the meal rites."

The *en*-priest dared too much. A king got his authority from his city's God through the *en*-priest or *nin*-priestess, but that did not give clerics the right to give kings orders. "Enkidu, get a cow." Gilgamesh shoved the priest aside and went in. The music halted, unevenly. The male and female priestesses stopped their ritual and stared at him. "Out! Out!" He stepped to the side and they pelted past him, food flying off trays and beer sloshing from pitchers.

Massive alabaster vases caught his attention, and he turned his blurred eyes on one. It showed the hierarchy of life. In the bottom row of carvings, water nourished plants, which nourished livestock. In the middle row, men carried offering, and in the top row they presented them to Inanna, who was surrounded by symbols of her authority.

A bearded man in a net skirt watched the offering ceremony, alone, ignored, irrelevant.

"This is how you see me?" He drove his shoulder into the vase. It spun halfway around, tipped, and crashed against the wall. A chunk of the edge cracked and fell to the floor. Shamhat moaned.

Gilgamesh made his way to Inanna Herself, kicking over the statuettes of Her worshippers as he approached. "You turned my people against me! Uruk is now a place of disorder. I blame You, pathetic self-proclaimed Queen of Heaven!" He spit on the ground in front of Her and shouted insults at every part of Her body from Her toes to Her genitals to the highest hair on Her head.

The *en*-priest threw himself in front of Inanna and flung his wrinkled old arms out wide as if to protect Her. "You aren't allowed in here, and the Goddess is hungry. Go home, Gilgamesh. Rest. Visit your wife and children. We'll talk tomorrow."

"Rebels greeted me at the wharf. We'll talk *now*."

Shamhat tugged on the *en*-priest's arm, but he would not budge. Annoyed lowing sounded behind him. Gilgamesh turned and saw Enkidu bumping against the doorway as he tried to push a cow in sideways. "Set it down, Enkidu. Aim its head this way, then give it a shove." Enkidu did as commanded, and the cow skittered into the room.

"Inanna is hungry, is She? Let's see if She likes what I feed Her." Gilgamesh grabbed the cow by the horns and gave its head a quick twist. As the corpse fell, he ripped off one horn and threw it at the Goddess, then the other. "Or maybe She'll like this better." He grabbed a hoof and tugged until the leg popped out of its socket and then ripped free. He threw it at the Goddess too. Nanna-Ur-Sag cringed but did not move from his position. "Enkidu, help me feed the Goddess." He slashed the cow's abdomen open with his knife and pulled out a warm, wet mass of intestines. "Enkidu!"

Enkidu instead picked up Shamhat and put her over one shoulder, and put the *en*-priest over the other. "Cows are grass-eaters." Tears ran down his face. "Until today, I protected grass-eaters. Now you make me part of one's death."

Even Enkidu had betrayed him. Gilgamesh lifted the intestines over his head and heaved them at the Goddess, more intestines pulling free from the abdomen as the mass flew through the air and splattered against the Goddess's face. His heartbeat pounded in his ears and head, and he bit his lip until he tasted blood.

He heard a moan and turned. Nanna-Ur-Sag and Shamhat peered around the corner of the door. "All the assassins are dead," Gilgamesh said flatly. Shamhat's hand flew to her mouth, but he heard the catch in her breath anyway. "Those who aren't already dead will be rounded up and executed." He smiled a bitter smile at Shamhat. "You're probably wondering which group your brother is in. Show up at my great house in two days and find out."

"Why not tomorrow? Why the wait?" Shamhat flung the words at him with unwomanly defiance.

"Tomorrow, Enkidu is king."

Chapter 26: Lord of Misrule

Uruk
The next morning
Enkidu, Gilgamesh

ENKIDU STROKED THE FUR ON THE LION SKIN, enjoying its coarseness and remembering how he had killed the lioness that wore the skin first. Today he would be shepherd again, this time of Uruk-the-Sheepfold. He would protect the people of Uruk against those who tried to hurt them.

Last night, Gilgamesh had been a lion in a sheepfold. Enkidu did not understand when or how things had changed.

But maybe they hadn't. Shamhat had told him in the desert Gilgamesh hurt harmless ones. But once they became brothers, he forgot.

He handed the skin to Gilgamesh, and the Wife of Gilgamesh undid the gold ribbons wound through Gilgamesh's hair and wove them into Enkidu's. "Today I am your king, brother? You follow my orders?"

Gilgamesh ground his teeth so loud Enkidu could hear them.

"Then I order you. Stay in the great house." Ordering felt good! "Play with your children. Tell your lady of our adventures. Send an offering to the shrine of Utu."

The Wife of Gilgamesh finished Enkidu's hair. She bent over and whispered, "Thank you." Enkidu left the great house and headed toward the Eanna. He had to talk to Shamhat. She would make sense of everything. But the guard at the gate told him she was at her brother's home.

The slave who greeted him the door looked terrified. "I won't hurt," Enkidu said. "I want to see Shamhat."

"No one's home." The slave's voice shook. Whispers hissed inside the house. Enkidu picked up the servant, set him aside, and followed his ears. In the inner courtyard he found Shamhat, a man who looked something like her, and another woman who was not as pretty but did smell strongly of beer. In the corner, an old woman wove cloth.

Shamhat threw herself in front of the man. "If you want to kill him, you'll have to kill me first."

Enkidu scratched his head, then looked at the man's face. He had been among the attackers who had run away. "Why did you want to hurt me? I'm Shamhat's friend."

"So Gilgamesh wasn't joking," Shamhat said, eyeing his hair ribbons. "You *are* king today."

"I want to be a good shepherd for my flock."

Shamhat looked at him the way a lamb looked at a wolf, then relaxed. She led him to a chair, sat on his lap, and kissed his cheek. "My sweet man. Always the protector. Will you protect me and my family now?"

Enkidu bared his teeth at the young man, who looked away. "Does this man threaten you?"

"No. He's my brother. Gilgamesh threatens us both."

"But—" Enkidu started, but Shamhat stroked his face.

"Please," she whispered.

He pulled her tighter against him. "I'll protect you."

She relaxed. She nestled against him with trust and love. "I brought you to Uruk to humble Gilgamesh. Remember? I told you he hurt his people instead of taking care of them." Her whisper in his ear made his arm fur stand up. "You are the better man. You should rule."

"Today I do."

"Yes, my king."

Her words made him feel big. Gilgamesh's words sometimes made him feel small. He was Gilgamesh's brother. Yet Gilgamesh chose what they would do. He didn't listen to Enkidu.

Shamhat continued. "People have been planning to overthrow Gilgamesh since before you came. I persuaded them to wait for you, their savior. But when you let Gilgamesh put you under his thumb—"

Enkidu growled. Shamhat laid soft fingers on his lips. "When you let Gilgamesh rule you, the people became afraid. Yesterday, some tried to overthrow Gilgamesh so the Gods wouldn't punish Uruk for Gilgamesh's sins."

"Your brother was there."

"Now Gilgamesh wants Geshtu to die."

Enkidu turned to Geshtu. "Why you want to hurt?"

"The king hurt my wife."

Enkidu looked at the woman scented with beer.

"No, Kirum's not my wife. My wife has returned to the clay. Because of Gilgamesh. She's buried beneath us."

"It's true," Shamhat said. Enkidu dug his nails into his hands. He looked down and saw the dirt floor had been dug up. A woman lay under there because of his brother. He put his hand to his forehead as a headache struck hard.

Geshtu continued. "When I was at the wharf, burning to punish the king, I became afraid. In my fear, my reason returned. It's not my place to punish the king, but the Gods'. I didn't want to sin. So I ran."

Enkidu understood why Geshtu came to the wharf. He also understood why he ran. Geshtu was no longer a danger. But last night Gilgamesh said he would kill those who ran away.

"Speak to Gilgamesh, my love," Shamhat begged. "He'll listen to you. Tell him the citizens fear he'll draw the Gods' wrath. Tell him the men at the wharf wanted the best for Uruk. Ask him to pardon those who changed their minds and ran. Tell him today, while you are king and he must listen to you. Call the council of old men to meet, and order Gilgamesh to listen to them. Will you do this for me?"

"Yes." He held her more tightly. She felt more rounded than before. He stroked her curves and wondered whether this house had a bed. "You're fat."

She pulled back. Her face turned red. "I'm going to have a baby."

"A little gazelle!" That would be wonderful, to be around a gazelle again. Then he remembered what she looked like without her clothes on, and worry hit him. "How will you feed it without an udder?"

She giggled, then stretched up and kissed him. "No, great king-for-today. *Your* child. A human baby. That's why Gilgamesh is angry with me."

His baby? How could that be? Then her final words hit him. "Gilgamesh doesn't want me to have a child?" The king had three human children plus the boy from An's temple who often visited. How could he begrudge Enkidu one?

He knew why. Gilgamesh wanted him to be the lesser always. He set Shamhat aside and stood. The pain in his head became unbearable. "I go." Shamhat called for him to wait, but anger turned his mind red. He must settle things with Gilgamesh now.

Gilgamesh had long ago tired of throwing the ball, but his sons still shrieked with joy as they ran about, trying as hard to bump into each other as they did to catch the ball. He would be happy when they grew big enough for real sport with him and Enkidu.

"I'm glad we can have you to ourselves for once."

He turned to his wife. She smiled at him as she sat under a potted palm and sewed.

"Enkidu's part of our family now."

Her smile changed to a pout. "Didn't the two of you get enough of each other's company on your quest? Didn't you miss me? Didn't you worry I might have been hurt in the attack?"

He snorted. "A few nomads. You weren't hurt. Now the citizens understand how my mere presence here protects them."

His lady leaned forward. "My lord, they think only of how scared they were and of the men who died fighting the nomads. They worry what would happen if the *Buranun* flooded without you here in charge. Even in the great house, I hear about it. The servants whisper; the guards talk about what to do next time you desert us."

"Desert you? Harsh—" Rough panting made him break off. Enkidu leaned against a pillar, thoroughly winded and bending over as if in pain.

Gilgamesh went to him, meaning to help him to a seat, but Enkidu shoved him away.

"I . . . challenge you . . . now. I . . . the better . . . man."

Gilgamesh put his arm around Enkidu's waist and staggered with him toward the bedroom. Enkidu had put on much weight since he first arrived. Lately, he got winded so easily, despite his great strength. And he was thirsty, always thirsty.

The journey had been hard on him, that was all. Enkidu needed to sleep in a bed and eat civilized food.

Gilgamesh laid Enkidu on his bed and arranged his limbs. Enkidu's arm shot up and grabbed Gilgamesh by the neck. "Leave Shamhat alone. My baby."

Gilgamesh peeled the fingers from his neck and then stroked Enkidu's hair. "Sleep now, lord king." His wife brought in a beaker of *kashbir*. Enkidu downed it quickly.

When at last Enkidu fell asleep, Gilgamesh's wife said, "Shamhat's child is Enkidu's? Is that why you took an interest in temple business?"

Gilgamesh stiffened, and panic hoarsened his throat. "It can't be Enkidu's. He's *my* friend, *my* soulmate."

His wife arched an eyebrow. "Perhaps *your* bed is not the only one he's been in."

"Silence, woman! Go to your children." She pressed her lips together, her shoulders stiffening. Then she dropped her gaze and left. When he could no longer hear her steps, he laid his head on Enkidu's chest and cried.

Chapter 27: At the Great House

Uruk
The next morning
Shamhat

KIRUM CLUNG TO SHAMHAT'S NECK, sobbing with grief. "Don't go. Don't leave me. Maybe the king will forget."

"Shh. You'll upset *Ama*." Last night, Shamhat had been in despair. She had prayed most of the night. This morning, she felt at peace and almost relieved. The world looked different, with crisper edges, brighter colors, and beauty in all things, even the beetles and cockroaches that skittered across the room at night.

She had wagered everything she cared about to free Uruk from its tyrant king. She had lost. She was tired of trying. Let Inanna find someone more worthy to set things right.

Geshtu came out of the bedroom combing his hair and adjusting the ankle-length linen skirt he had bought for the occasion. "Maybe Enkidu talked the king out of punishing us."

"Probably," Shamhat said to cheer Kirum and Geshtu. But she doubted it. Many times Enkidu had promised her he would do this or that. But never had the city benefited. She doubted Enkidu ever said anything. He was too besotted with his "brother."

Geshtu rubbed his temples. "Let's go. I don't want us mocked as cowards. Shamhat, I forgive you."

"For what?" She had many sins to account for.

"Your womanhood belonged to this family until we gave it to Inanna, and then it belonged to the temple. You dishonored me and Inanna by sharing what was not yours with Enkidu."

Shamhat bowed her head. "I believed I did Inanna's will."

Geshtu touched Kirum on the shoulder. "Don't worry, Kirum. I won't say a word about your helping the resistance, even under torture."

Kirum wailed, and Shamhat struggled to disentangle herself. "If neither of us come back, you'll watch over *Ama*?" Kirum promised again, and Shamhat pulled free. "Geshtu, let's go meet our destiny, as befits our rank and family." They left together, walking hand in hand and not looking back at the house their family had lived in for generations.

Shamhat stood on her tiptoes, trying to see over the crowd. Dozens of people waited at the gates to the great house, but they remained shut. "Can you tell what's happening?"

"No." Geshtu looked around, then spoke in a low voice. "I don't see any of the men from the attack on the king. You and I appear to be the only ones coming to be executed."

Shamhat trembled and she held Geshtu's hand tighter to keep from running away. "Don't say that! The Gods may have moved the king to mercy."

"Or Enkidu. Gilgamesh pays more attention to him than to the Gods." Geshtu tapped the shoulder of the sun-blackened man with a shaved head in front of him. "Excuse me. Do you know what's going on?"

The man turned and rolled his eyes. "I doubt Inanna Herself knows what's happening in this place. A week ago I couldn't get a permit for trading because the king was away desecrating Enlil's sacred cedar forest. Yesterday I couldn't get a permit because a wild man had the throne for the day. Today, who knows? Perhaps sheep rule."

An elderly man whose chest sagged like an old woman's turned around. "I heard someone in the royal family is sick."

"I heard the king has gone mad."

"The king was already mad," Geshtu muttered. Shamhat elbowed him. As morning became afternoon, grumbling hungry

162

people left to get food, and others simply left. The bald, dark-skinned trader tried to start several conversations with them, but gave up after their terse answers. Eventually, complaining, he forced his way to the front and spoke with the guards. Then he walked away without passing Shamhat and Geshtu.

Shamhat had started the day ready for whatever punishment the king and the *en*-priest gave her. But as her shadow grew short, disappeared, and then grew long again, her resignation gave way to panic that increased the longer they waited. The heat of the summer sun took its toll, and she became woozy, and her lips cracked. She had the heat-mad thought that the king planned to execute them by letting them bake to death.

A priestess who had left the crowd earlier returned with a bowl of lentils cooked with onions and dressed with oil, and the luscious aroma reawakened Shamhat's desire to live. A tavernkeeper wove through the crowd with beakers of *ebla*, and the yeasty smell made Shamhat long for the days when she was an ordinary priestess who kept the rituals of the temple and her little brother was a carefree man about to be married.

Babati waded into the remaining crowd. "Go home!" he shouted. "Come back tomorrow." Grumbling, the people dispersed. Shamhat took a step and her knees gave way. Geshtu caught her. She shook like a baby bird.

"The gift of a day. Inanna heard your prayers, Sister. Why are you so undone?"

"I've used up all my bravery."

"Never. You went into the desert and tamed a wild man. You can find your courage again," he encouraged her. "I'll stop at Kirum's tavern and get whatever beer you want. Your bravery may be waiting at the bottom of a *kuli*."

The thought of passing the slow hours until she knew her fate drunk tempted her. She wanted so much to agree. "No." She sighed and pulled her hand from his. "I should go to the Eanna and put the records in order for whoever takes my place." They separated. Shamhat had walked only a few arms' lengths before Babati's shout stopped her.

"Not you, Shamhat."

In spite of the blistering dry-season heat, cold enveloped her like a desert night. Citizens turned to stare. One looked at her belly and mouthed the word "whore." Another muttered, "She's a trough from which the pigs eat."

For now, she still wore the headdress of a priestess of Inanna. She straightened her backbone, lifted her chin high, and followed Babati with majesty even the Wife of Gilgamesh could not match.

The Wife of Gilgamesh looked at Shamhat through narrowed, sleep-deprived eyes, then barked a bitter laugh. "You're surprised I sent for you."

"Great lady, I thought the king wanted to punish me." Shamhat could not release her tight fists. It was probably for the good; she would shake all over if she did.

"Yesterday, certainly." She cast a reproachful gaze at Shamhat's belly. "But things have changed. Come." The Wife of Gilgamesh led her to the king's bedchamber. The room smelled of sweetness and vomit, and Enkidu lay on the bed, sweating, his eyes half-closed. Gilgamesh huddled next to him on the bed, frowning.

"Why'd you bring that onyx-eyed harlot in here?" he shouted. "Enkidu is fine."

The Wife of Gilgamesh flinched. "A priestess should hear his dream and pray for him."

Gilgamesh's face reddened at his wife's presumption. Enkidu's eyes opened and he said weakly, "Shamhat?"

She didn't wait for the king's approval. She ran to him. "I'm here."

"I'm afraid."

"No! It was a false dream." Gilgamesh glared at Shamhat as if to warn her not to contradict him.

"Tell me your dream." Shamhat stroked Enkidu's hot cheek.

"The Gods sat in council to judge us, Gilgamesh and me. An said to the others, 'These two deserve punishment. They killed Humbaba. They chopped down the sacred trees of the Cedar Forest. One must die. Who shall it be?'

"Inanna spoke on my behalf. 'My priestess tamed Enkidu with My arts. He belongs to Me. As queen of heaven, I say spare him.'

"Utu spoke for Gilgamesh. 'The king has long been under my protection. Spare Gilgamesh.'

"The Gods then looked to Enlil because the Cedar Forest had belonged to him. He said, 'I collected the *me*, the holy foundation stones of civilization, and gave them to Enki to share with *all* the cities. But Inanna, You got Enki drunk, and he gave You the *me*. You gave them to Uruk and made it foremost of all cities. You took what was not Yours. Now, You who style Yourself queen of heaven, We take what is Yours. Enkidu is the one who will die.'

"Then I woke, sick." He moaned as he struggled to change position. "Surely I was born on an ill-fated day."

Shamhat patted his head. "Rest now, Enkidu. I will pray in the courtyard for you and burn cedar for Bau." Her stomach fluttered with panic. Enkidu was truly sick. His breath smelled sweet and fruity like a spoiled apple, but underneath lingered the scent of decay.

Enkidu caught her hand as she stood. "Will my baby be big and tall like me?"

His hand was bigger than it had been when they first met. Her stomach twisted from worry and hunger, and she couldn't laugh at his childlike question. "The baby will start out tiny. But it will grow over time, as a gazelle fawn would." Gilgamesh's face grew darker. "May I go pray?" The king waved her away, and the Wife of Gilgamesh followed her.

"Well?"

Shamhat smoothed her braid with a shaking hand. "Great Lady, I fear his dream might be true. I think you should send for a physician from the temple of An." The Wife of Gilgamesh clapped her hands twice for a servant.

Shamhat and the Wife of Gilgamesh sat silently in the private courtyard until the physician arrived, followed by his scribe. Shamhat told him about the smell of Enkidu's breath.

The physician strode into the king's bedroom with Shamhat and the scribe trailing and sniffed Enkidu's breath himself. He frowned. "Is he unusually thirsty?" he asked. "Has he been pissing often?"

"Yes, until today," Gilgamesh said. "Today, he vomited and wasn't hungry."

"The chamber pot." The scribe picked it up, and the physician sniffed.

"Good news. He does not have a plague."

"Then what's wrong?" Gilgamesh demanded.

"Pray over him twelve times each day. After each prayer have him drink a beaker of water that's been boiled and cooled."

"When will he get up from the bed?" Gilgamesh asked.

The physician's gaze shifted away. "Only the Gods can cure. I pray my instructions will make him more comfortable."

"Then what use are you?" Gilgamesh roared and took several steps toward the physician. "Get out! Take your false remedies." The physician ran, tangling his feet in his long skirt, and Gilgamesh hurled the chamber pot at him, hitting him square in the back. "You too, Shamhat! I never want to see you again. Go!"

As she ran, she heard Enkidu call her name.

Five days later, Shamhat prayed, as customary, before beginning work on accounts, but the voices of the other scribes distracted her, and she made the symbol for "ug," death, instead of the one for "ag," which marked possession. "Quiet!" she said, setting down her reed in annoyance. She had to do a good job so the *en*-priest would not regret welcoming her back to the temple. Nanna-Ur-Sag forbade her to serve in worship, but he had not sent her away yet. He said as long as Enkidu lived, he might yet humble the king.

She wet her thumb and wiped the clay to erase her mistake. Already, the other scribes gossiped. She could hardly blame them. She had not only been listening to rumors, she had also sought them out. If even some of them proved true, it boded ill for Uruk. Enkidu lay close to death. Enkidu had died. Enkidu had gotten well and left the city. The king ranted and raved and no one could go near him, not even his wife or mother.

Men who had come to Kirum's tavern before to talk revolt now did so again. One good thing had come of Enkidu's illness: The king appeared to have forgotten about the rebellion. Geshtu waited each day in his best clothes for a summons, pacing and giving Dabta final instructions until the slave must be able to recite them in unison. No summons ever came. Shamhat had slipped out this morning to visit him and found him at his workbench carving cylinder seals.

The other scribes went silent, and Shamhat looked up. Nanna-Ur-Sag stood in the doorway. "Shamhat, you have a summons from the king."

When Shamhat arrived at the great house, Babati led her immediately to the king's bedroom. What had been an unpleasant smell before was now an intolerable stench that made her retch, yet the king and his wife appeared to have been there for some time. Bowls of uneaten food sat next to each of them. Enkidu lay with his eyes closed, struggling for breath. Her stomach turned over. He was deathly ill.

"You sent for me, lord king?"

Gilgamesh's mouth twisted in displeasure. "Enkidu asked for you."

Shamhat sat on the bed and leaned close to Enkidu. "I'm here, love."

He struggled to open his eyes. She expected to see fear there, or affection, or puzzlement.

What she didn't expect was hate.

"Curse you all!"

His foul breath reminded her of Nameshda's open grave. She tried to draw back, but he grabbed her arm. "Utu, great patron of Gilgamesh and lord of the sun, I call on you. I was healthy and happy in the wilderness.

"I would still be running free if Zaidu the trapper had not found me. May his traps always be empty.

"I would still be running free if Shamhat the priestess had not tamed me. May she be forced from the temple; may she make her living in a tavern.

"Utu, may Zaidu never know happiness in the wilderness. May Shamhat never know happiness in the city."

Shamhat sucked in her breath. "You were a filthy creature who lived like an animal and couldn't speak! Because of me, you've tasted beer and bread, and you've known the love of a woman and of a brother."

Enkidu licked his lips, and his eyes gazed in different directions.

Shamhat fought her tears. He had been a sweet man and an enthusiastic pupil. That he left her with a curse instead of a kiss tore at her liver. "I'm the mother of your child!"

"Shamhat, may all I've prayed come to pass for seducing me with the wiles of Inanna. Go away." He released her arm.

Shamhat's dry mouth tasted of ashes. "Enkidu, you're not thinking straight. Please, take away your curse. Everything good in your life is because of me."

"Everything bad as well," Gilgamesh growled. "It would have been better I had never had him than to see him suffer like this. Go, Shamhat. I want nothing of your evil in my house."

Babati pulled her gently to her feet and led her from the room. She took one last look at Enkidu and called to him. "Please!"

Enkidu turned away.

Chapter 28: Death Comes for All

The wilderness
Late that afternoon
Zaidu

Z AIDU'S SHADOW WAS LONG LIKE THE DAYS. The cool promise of the coming evening lessened the blistering blaze of the summer sun. He picked up the shovel and began his task.

Near the skin that had served so long as a tent, he thrust the shovel into the hard, crusty sand, lifted it out, and swiveled to dump the contents behind him. He struck again and again, each time removing a little more dirt. After a while his muscles ached from the unfamiliar motion, but he welcomed the pain. He focused on its pulse, its sharpness, how it snapped like a bow with each stroke and then ebbed.

"Good health to you!"

Zaidu swung at the voice, holding the shovel in front of him like a weapon and cursing himself. He hadn't been paying attention. What if it had been a lion?

"I'm looking for the shepherds who camped nearby. They promised me some plucked wool in exchange for goods from the city." He had a shaved head, like a city man, but his skin was burned dark, like Zaidu's own. His donkey sagged under its burden. He looked like the trader he claimed to be.

Zaidu kept his shovel raised anyway. "When the dry season started, they moved their flock closer to the river."

"Ah." The trader surveyed Zaidu's own goods. "That's a fine gazelle skin you're wearing. Would you take a copper bowl for it?"

Zaidu let his arm drop. "I'm busy. I need to finish this hole before it's dark."

"What if I help? Later, we can discuss what you might want to trade." The man rummaged around in his baskets and took out a copper shovel head. "Do you have a reed?"

Zaidu handed him one, and they dug together. At last the hole was deep enough. They stood next to each other and contemplated their work, panting from their labors.

"What will you do now?" the trader asked.

"I don't know. Keep trapping, I guess."

"Well, whatever you do, stay clear of Uruk. The city is in an uproar."

Uruk. Shamhat's city. "Why?"

"The king adopted a wild man as a brother. When I was there several days ago, the wild man was dying. He's probably returned to the clay by now. The government shut down while the king sat with his wild man, and men talked openly in the street of revolt."

Shamhat was in danger. Alarm penetrated his deadened feelings and the fog in his mind. "I do have things to trade, including this gazelle skin. Do you have a fleece skirt like the city men wear?"

The trader's face brightened. "I'm sure I can make you a good deal. But shouldn't we finish your task first?"

Zaidu gripped the reed handle of his shovel so hard it cracked. He opened his hand and let the pieces fall. He looked at his hand. New blisters grew on top of years-old callouses. He looked at the hole. "Yes," he answered the trader.

Together, they lifted *Ada*'s body, carried it to the hole, and gently placed it inside.

Chapter 29: Shooting Star

Uruk
Several days later
Gilgamesh, Shamhat, Gilgamesh

GILGAMESH OPENED HIS EYES, and the slanted pink light of dawn made him squint. Morning already? He'd promised Enkidu he wouldn't sleep or eat until he was well, but so many nights of no sleep had forced him to break his promise.

He rolled over and was glad to see Enkidu still slumbered and had not noticed his lapse. His wife slept too, curled in a ball like a child. "Enkidu, wake up. Utu has sent the sun into the sky again." Enkidu didn't stir. "Enkidu!" Gilgamesh said louder. His wife woke and rubbed her eyes. Gilgamesh shook Enkidu. His arm was alabaster—pale, hard, cold.

Lifeless.

He snatched his hand back. "What trick is this? Don't play games, dearest brother."

His lady rose and came around the bed to him. She put her soft, plump arms around his neck. She laid her cheek on his head and spoke softly. "He is dead, great king. We must have him prepared for burial."

Gilgamesh waited for Enkidu to laugh, to look up, to say, "I was holding my breath and pretending." He brushed a strand of Enkidu's hair from his face. "We can't bury him yet. He may still be alive."

His wife spoke to him as if he were a child. "He has truly returned to the clay. We must plan his funeral."

He pulled away from the comfort of her arms and looked at her coldly. "There are no 'musts' when kings are involved. Only my word is a 'must.'"

She stood and gave him a haughty look. "I am the daughter of a king, the sister of a king, the wife of a king, and, Inanna and the council of old men willing, the mother of a king. This is a royal household, and I will run it properly. I won't let your people or your enemies think you a fool."

"My brother will wake."

"Give me your cylinder seal. I will hide your madness, for the sake of Uruk and my sons." He put up no resistance as she slipped the chain from his neck. He waited until she left the room. Then he lay next to Enkidu and put his hand on Enkidu's chest, waiting to feel his breath.

A week later, the Wife of Gilgamesh waved the king's seal in front of Shamhat. "Your brother is under a death sentence. As long as I have this seal, I can commute it. But you have to make me some promises."

The dense cloud of fragrant smoke made Shamhat cough. "Please tell me, great lady. Is Enkidu alive? May I see him?"

The Wife of Gilgamesh lifted a eyebrow. "You still care for him, after he cursed you?"

Shamhat clasped her hands tightly, trying to read the answers to her questions in the eyes of the Wife of Gilgamesh. "I led him by the hand like a little child and taught him the ways of civilization. He was more my son than my own son can ever be. He's the father of my child. A few words uttered in madness can't destroy love."

The Wife of Gilgamesh rolled her eyes. "Will you make promises to me to save your brother?" Her fingernails clicked on her armrest.

Shamhat's stomach fell. How could she bear to sacrifice any more? Then she remembered her time in the desert. After that, she could brave anything, endure anything. She would do whatever it took to save Geshtu. "Yes, great lady."

The Wife of Gilgamesh relaxed. "I like that you thought so long. I believe you will keep your word. I will write an order banishing your brother. He must never come back to Uruk." She pointed to a second clay tablet. "In return, you must deliver this letter imprinted with the king's seal to the *en*-priest. It orders him to remove you as priestess."

Shamhat took a step back, and her hands clenched. The price of her brother's life was steep.

"My spies told me your brother encouraged the men at Kirum's tavern to defy their king. He's a scorpion whose stinger must be removed."

Shamhat fell to her knees. "You speak wisely, great lady. But if I leave the temple, I'll never have an excuse to see Inanna-Ama-Mu again. I beg you, will you adopt him, so I'll know a mother looks out for him?"

"Don't push your luck, priestess. If I adopt the boy, the king may look upon him more favorably than his other sons. No, I'll break his contract with the temple, and you can have him, as long as Gilgamesh never sees him again. When Gilgamesh looks for a successor, I want his eyes to fall on *my* sons."

Shamhat lowered her face so the Wife of Gilgamesh could not see how joy leaped in her liver. Inanna-Ama-Mu would at last know her as his mother.

"I have another task for you." The Wife of Gilgamesh paced the courtyard. "Enkidu returned to the clay seven days ago. The king refuses to believe he is dead. He has dressed him in fine clothes and takes him food and beer. When Enkidu started to stink, Gilgamesh anointed him with expensive oils and started burning herbs and cedar day and night. Enkidu must have a funeral and be buried. But the king will not listen to me. Meanwhile, I neglect my own fields and workers while caring for his duties and hiding that he is deranged."

"I doubt the king will listen to me."

"You know the love-arts of Inanna. Clearly you are expert at manipulating men with Her wiles." She glared at Shamhat's heavy belly, which now pressed, rounded, against her linen gown. "Bring the king back to his right mind. Make him ready to wear this seal again.

Then leave by the other door. I never want to see you and your seductress's eyes again."

"You'll send an order to the house of An about Inanna-Ama-Mu?"

"Yes."

"You'll have my gratitude always, great lady. Thank you for my brother's life and my son." She rose and went toward the king's bedroom, filled with dread about what she would find.

The light footsteps of a woman entered the bedroom. "Go away, wife. I won't listen to your lies."

Fabric rustled. "It's I, Shamhat. Once, I was Inanna and you were Dumuzi in the Sacred Marriage. Let me again be your friend."

The sultry voice sent shivers down his spine. Gilgamesh looked up through a blur of tears. The priestess knelt nearby, her head down, as beautiful and alluring as ever. "My wife sent you to seduce me."

"Yes."

"You can't separate me from Enkidu."

She lifted her head, stood, and came and sat by the bed without asking his permission. In her serious face, her eyes sparkled like obsidian, drawing him in despite himself. Her walk was more a waddle because of the load she bore, reminding him she had stolen some of his short time with Enkidu.

"Leave us!" he shouted.

She remained sitting. "My king, hear me out. Have I not always followed your orders, even to the point of dishonor?"

He would have to leave Enkidu to throw her out, and he wouldn't call the servants to do it. He wanted no one here with him and Enkidu. "Be brief."

"Think of your legacy. Right here in Uruk, you can roll your seal on history and have your name live forever. Repair the temples. Prod the lazy priests and priestesses to celebrate all the rites the Gods are due. Reward good and punish wrongdoing. Raise your boys so they know how to be great kings." She leaned forward and brought her hands together as if praying. "I beg you, put your childish ways behind and be the great man I know you are inside. Strive for wisdom."

"What insolence! Who are you to criticize my rule? Get out."

Again she disobeyed. "I'll write new praise poems about you. Gilgamesh, you are in the favor of Utu. Wear his light brightly."

"When Enkidu awakes," he said to get her to leave.

She looked at him with pitying eyes. "No one could love Enkidu as much as you did, but I did love him. If I prove he has left you, will you listen?"

Gilgamesh shook his head. He could not listen to her. She would trick him with reason and soft words. She lowered herself heavily onto the bed. She lifted the cloth he had laid across Enkidu's face to keep the flies from annoying him.

She pointed to Enkidu's nose. "Look, my lord. Enkidu is filled with worms."

"No." Gilgamesh turned his head away. Shamhat took hold of his chin and turned it, forcing him to look. It could not be a worm. Enkidu merely needed to blow his nose. "No," he said again. She kept the pressure on his chin. To his horror, the thing coming out of Enkidu's nose wiggled down to his lips.

He recoiled in horror, and vomit burned his throat. "No!" The room echoed with his cry of pain. "Lord Utu, no!" He shook like wet laundry shaken by a servant in the courtyard. He fell against Shamhat, weeping.

He wept until he had no more tears, but still his chest heaved with grief. Grief was both a stone that weighed his shoulders down and a hollowness like hunger, a hunger that could never be sated. He was alone. In his teeming city, in his great house, with his family and Shamhat, he was alone. It was as if the thinnest of linen hung before his eyes. He was part of the world, and yet separate from it forever.

At last Gilgamesh lifted his head. Tears spilled from Shamhat's eyes. It was something, a connection, that she too felt his loss. "I am stripped to nothing," he admitted.

Shamhat's expression went from surprise to understanding. "When I went to the wilderness, I abandoned my headdress, my beads of lapis lazuli, my beads of abalone, my face paints, my cylinder seal, my beaded belt, my sandals. I was stripped of everything that made me who I am, everything I thought made life worth living. Great king, can you guess what I discovered?"

"That like me, you were nothing."

"No, great king. I discovered I still existed. Like Inanna, I descended to the Netherworld and I rose again, changed but still Shamhat." She leaned closer to him, her face intense. "Gilgamesh and Shamhat are more than their roles!"

Her words made no sense. Gilgamesh the king and Gilgamesh the slave could never be the same. In the New Year's festivities, he was Dumuzi, and the rest of the year he wasn't. Roles defined people.

He had been Enkidu's brother and now he wasn't. Enkidu gave his life meaning and now he had no meaning.

He shook his head. "You're wrong. What you say goes against the natural ranking of people the Gods instituted."

She stroked his face. "Don't you recognize any piece in you of the old Gilgamesh?"

He closed his eyes, emptied his thoughts, and sought for something that was not emptiness. He found . . . himself. He was still there, battered and warped like a copper pot that had been kicked down the street, but still could be cooked in. The knowledge sliced like a knife.

"What will I do without Enkidu? He was the other half of me, my brother."

"Rule your city wisely, serve the Gods, take comfort in your family, and raise your boys to be kings."

He stroke Enkidu's head. "Once I lusted for glory. Once I cared nothing for danger and death, as long as my name lived on. But look at Enkidu. A mighty man, with the strength of twenty. Yet now he is worm food."

"Everyone dies, my king." Her shaking hand picked at the fringe of her shawl.

"Utnapishtim didn't die."

"He and his wife saved the creatures of the earth in their boat when Enlil tried to drown creation in a great flood. Can you claim so great a feat?" She squeezed his hand. "Enjoy life while you have it. Too soon, we will be like Enkidu."

Gilgamesh rested his forehead in his hands. "How can I enjoy life? I see Enkidu lying there, and I shake with terror. As great as my sorrow for Enkidu is, even greater is my sorrow that I, too, must one day die."

"Only the Gods live forever. We work for Them for a time and then we rest."

"I can't bear it. Nothing is meaningful if Enkidu is dead and death awaits me. My wife is no joy, my children no treasure. Even your beauty doesn't arouse my lust." He looked around the room. Colors seemed muted and lines, fuzzy. His gold and silver lacked sparkle.

Shamhat crinkled her eyebrows. "My king, you must accept death. We all must. It is our fate."

Gilgamesh shook his head. "It won't be mine. I will find Utnapishtim and learn the secret of eternal life. Go now, Shamhat, and remember me in your prayers."

Still she disobeyed. "This isn't the purpose I hoped you would choose. Please, think again."

"No. This is my purpose now."

She hesitated, then kissed his forehead and left the room.

With a sigh, Gilgamesh heaved himself to his feet. He went to the lamp that had burnt out days ago, wiped his fingers around the edge, and drew lines on his face with the soot. He pulled the gold and silver ribbons from his hair and shook his head upside down to tangle his hair. He took off his gold earrings, his many chains, the jeweled rings he wore on every finger, his jeweled sandals, his embroidered skirt.

This time, he would leave the city prepared. He would give his seal to the council of elders to rule in his absence and to care for the temples and the Gods. He would charge the council of young men with protecting the city.

He went to the cedar chest under the window. He had been so proud of it. The top was inlaid with squares and diamonds of lapis, carnelian, and abalone, and its front had an inlay showing him killing a lion.

Now he valued the chest only for what it held. He lifted the lid and tenderly lifted out the lion skin. He had won this from Enkidu. He would wear it on his quest.

He wrapped it around him and secured it with rude pins of bronze.

Chapter 30: All Things End

Uruk
Later that day
Shamhat

"ENKIDU HAS HUMBLED THE KING."
Shamhat knelt in front of the *en*-priest in the archives, crying unashamedly. *Ada*'s death had not caused her such agony. Inanna had accomplished Her purpose, but she and Enkidu had paid dearly. "Gilgamesh will no longer terrorize the city."

"Finally!" Nanna-Ur-Sag rocked, his hands locked in prayer. "Then my dream was true, and you did act as Inanna wanted. Your actions are blameless."

His words salved her grief and guilt. Inanna wanted her child to be. Unfortunately, others would still consider her to have sinned. She handed Nanna-Ur-Sag the tablet the Wife of Gilgamesh had signed with the king's seal, the tablet that ordered the *en*-priest to dismiss her.

Enkidu's curse still weighed on her. Taverns offered two jobs for women, and she did not know how to brew beer.

Nanna-Ur-Sag finished reading. He turned to the shelves and rearranged some tablets. "You deserve to be restored to your previous role." He cleared his throat, obviously embarrassed and distressed. "You would be if it were up to me, my daughter."

"I know what the letter says. I'll pack my things and go quietly." She stood. "You've been like a father to me. You'll be in my prayers always."

He shook his head. "I'll talk to the king. Maybe I can persuade him to change his mind."

"It'll do no good. Besides, my brother is in disgrace. If I stayed, I would taint the temple."

She could see in his face he knew she spoke the truth. At last he nodded and took a tablet off of the shelf. "One of the scribes filed this. It's not appropriate for a temple archive. Take it as a memory of your time here and of how you saved Uruk from the king's misdeeds."

The tablet was misshapen and twisted. She took it and read out loud, sounding out the stretched symbols with effort. "Like Inanna's reed doorpost, upright and tall is he. Like Inanna, he protects the weak." She stopped, blushing. Her praise poem about Enkidu. "Thank you, Nanna-Ur-Sag."

He put his hand on her shoulder. "You look worried and weary."

She nodded.

"You must radiate joy and sensuality always, as you were trained. You will always be a priestess of Inanna, even if you're not at the temple. It is part of you. You embody the Goddess."

Geshtu was drunk when Shamhat arrived home, carrying her belongings in baskets, Inanna-Ama-Mu at her side. The boy was confused yet defiant, and she had had to half-drag him. Not a good start for their new relationship.

Geshtu looked at her with bleary eyes. "I've had no customers. Not a single one. Kirum says the word in her tavern is that no one wants to take a chance of paying me for a seal I won't finish because I'm dead." He lifted his *kuli* to his mouth, but it was empty. "I might as well be dead. How will I earn a living, let alone save up a bride price for a new wife? I paid Nur-Ea back the dowry, but he refuses to return the bride price."

Shamhat thought of the old proverb, "Fate is a dog, well able to bite." She dropped her baskets. "You have more troubles than that." She gestured at her clothes, a simple undecorated robe with no sash. "I'm no longer a priestess of Inanna and I've brought disgrace to the family. I've also been cursed in the name of Utu. I have nowhere to go but here, and I've brought my son with me." Geshtu looked at her without comprehension. "I do have one good piece of news. You've been pardoned." She handed him the tablet the Wife had signed with the king's seal.

He didn't ask her to read it. "Pardoned? I'm not going to be executed?"

"No."

He let out a whoop and stood unsteadily. "Then I'm going to celebrate. At every tavern, with every beaker of beer, I'll praise the king's name."

Shamhat took his arm. "Don't celebrate yet." He was as selfish as ever. He thought only of his pardon and not of her or Inanna-Ama-Mu. Enkidu had been like marsh grass, swaying this way and that. Gilgamesh had had a restless *zi*, always seeking—first excitement, then glory, now eternal life. Three men, all flawed, all bound to her by the Gods. "Geshtu, there's more. You've been banished. You must leave Uruk forever."

He put his palm to his forehead, his eyes suddenly clear. "What are we to do?"

Shamhat had no idea.

Shamhat slept restlessly that night, tossing and turning, the words of the curse burning in her mind. Part had already come true: She'd been forced from the temple.

The second part was that she would make her living in a tavern. Her prospects were indeed bleak. She doubted anyone would hire a disgraced priestess as a scribe or, for that matter, would want her as a wife. She might end up standing against the wall of a tavern, smiling at the men, after all. No, she would do anything to avoid that. But there was still the third part of the curse to consider, that she would never be happy.

Worst of all, she had no say in her fate. Now she'd left the temple, her younger brother had the authority to decide what became of her and her children. Legally, she was property to be disposed of.

She rose, dressed, and went to sit in the inner courtyard. Dabta was already up, repositioning furniture that had no need to be moved. "Will I be sold?" he asked quietly.

She leaned her head against the chair. "That's in Geshtu's hands. As is my fate and my son's. Go to the tavern and see whether Kirum is up. If she is, ask her to come eat with us. Then cook our morning meal."

By the time Kirum arrived, the rest of the family had joined Shamhat. They would have a family meeting, just as when *Ada* lived. Kirum sat next to Shamhat and held her hand. "Does the king know my tavern served as a meeting place?"

"I think so."

"Then I'll be in trouble next." Her voice shook.

Geshtu cleared his throat. "Shamhat, you know the most about the other cities. Which would most need a cylinder seal maker? Kish?"

Kirum spoke instead. "King Aga of Kish is weak, or so the traders in my tavern say. They claim Ur is growing, and its king is strong."

"Kish is far upriver," Shamhat added. "It would be a long walk for *Ama*."

Geshtu shifted in his chair. "You and *Ama* will stay in this house. I'm taking only Dabta."

Shamhat threw her hands up. "You're not thinking, little brother. The king will confiscate our—your—house. What then?"

"I'm the law in this house." Geshtu puffed up, full of his authority, and Shamhat bit her lip, expecting another lecture on her proper place.

"You should all move together." Everyone looked at Kirum. "Families belong together. You are lucky to have each other. Besides, there is nothing left for you here, Shamhat, but disgrace."

"Come with us," Shamhat said impulsively. "You'll be safe, and a breweress is welcome anywhere."

Geshtu pounded his fist on the table as *Ada* used to do. "I haven't said you and *Ama* are coming with me. And Kirum, what about your love-struck fisherman?"

Kirum blushed and looked away. "He disapproved of my friendship with your family."

Her loyalty made Shamhat feel stronger. She said quietly, "Breweresses are desirable wives. You'll find another man soon." Geshtu looked at Kirum as if he'd never seen her before.

Kirum said, "Shamhat, I could teach you how to brew and run a tavern. Then you could support yourself and your children."

"May she make her living in a tavern," Enkidu had said in his curse. With Kirum's help, she could do so as a breweress, not a prostitute. She leaned forward, taut as a bowstring, afraid to hope. Kirum's suggestion would be best for everyone.

Geshtu scratched his head, Inanna-Ama-Mu fidgeted, and Kirum scrunched her skirt in her hand.

"If we all went together—if—we still need a plan and a place to go," Geshtu said. His mask of household head cracked, and Shamhat could tell he found his role terrifying.

Steps sounded in the entry. A familiar voice called, "Shamhat?" Shamhat's ears filled with the roar of blood.

Shamhat stood, trembling so hard she had to grasp the back of the chair. "I'm here."

A man walked in the door, and she drooped with disappointment. This was a city man, with curled hair, a shaved face, and a spotless fleece skirt. He smelled of scented oil.

"A client for you, Geshtu."

"I'm sorry, but you're too late. We're leaving the city," Geshtu said.

The man looked at Shamhat from beneath arrow-straight brows, and his smile grew. "You don't recognize me, do you?"

Shamhat stepped closer. "Zaidu? It is you!" Her arms wrapped around him before she could stop them. Here was the one man in her life who hadn't let her down. When her belly bumped him, he stiffened, and Shamhat pulled away. "Enkidu returned to the clay. My baby is fatherless." She pretended to brush dust from her robe. "Have you chosen city life?"

"I thought I might try it out." His smile faded. "But you're busy moving. Perhaps I should go."

Shamhat grabbed the chair back. Zaidu had evaded Enkidu's curse! By coming to the city, it didn't matter if his traps failed or he was unhappy in the desert.

If Zaidu could avoid the fate the curse decreed, perhaps she could too. Her legs threatened to give, and she wobbled.

Kirum looked between Zaidu and Shamhat and then grinned at Shamhat. "Come with us, Shamhat's friend," she said. "Like you, we're starting new lives."

"First things first. I still haven't decided where we're going or who's going," Geshtu grumbled.

The third part of the curse said Shamhat would never be happy *in the city.* Zaidu would never be happy in the wilderness. They needed to be somewhere that was neither. "I know a place. It could use a breweress, a priestess, and a trapper, and Geshtu, you'd be close enough to the city to still sell your cylinder seals."

Geshtu pressed his lips together in anger at her impertinence, then shook his head and leaned back. "You'll always be the older sister, won't you? Spit it out. Where is this place so perfect?"

"It's called Uzarali."

Chapter 31: New Beginnings

Uzarali
Two years later
Shamhat

ALL NEWS CAME TO UZARALI SOONER OR LATER, Shamhat had learned. Today's news stunned and delighted her. According to a trader, King Gilgamesh had returned from his quest a chastened and humble man, a man at last willing to devote his tremendous energy and strength to his city.

Now seemed the time to start the poem Inanna had commanded her in a dream to write. She had waited for the theme, which Inanna used today's news to reveal.

Shamhat checked that her youngest daughter still slept. Zaidu had taken the other two children fishing. She picked up the clay and kneaded it, her hands still remembering the motions. Then she sliced the end from a reed and wrote the first two stanzas.

"Uruk, city beyond equal,
"Mighty Uruk, first of cities,
"Where dwells Inanna, Goddess of Love,
"Where dwells Inanna, Goddess of War,
"In the great jeweled temple,
"Surrounded by gardens,
"Ruled by the just and wise King Gilgamesh
"Most powerful of men.

"Read now of the salvation of Uruk,
"Uruk, the holy house of Inanna.
"Once the king, Gilgamesh, oppressed his people,
"Took what was not his, raged like a bull.
"But the Gods sent a wild man, a companion to the king.
"Enkidu's death humbled Gilgamesh.
"Uruk, city beyond equal,
"Mighty Uruk, first of cities."

Author's Note

What do we know of the historical Gilgamesh? His name appears as king of Uruk on a list of kings of Sumer, where he is credited with ruling one hundred twenty-six years.

All else is myth.

The "Epic of Gilgamesh" as we now know it was composed in roughly 1200 BCE—some fifteen hundred years after the fact—by a Babylonian priest named Sîn-lēqi-unninni. As a result, many of its details, including behavior and clothes, date to Babylonian times, not to Gilgamesh's era. Although many earlier fragments exist, some quite different, I took my inspiration from Stephen Mitchell's rendering of Sîn-lēqi-unninni's version, while inventing most of the characters and plot.

Uruk. Uruk was indeed the greatest city of the ancient world. Encircled by a wall that still in some places stands sixteen feet tall, Uruk in its glory—probably shortly before Gilgamesh's time—covered two square miles and housed as many as eighty thousand people. Not until Imperial Rome did a city match it.

Because only five percent of Uruk has been excavated, primarily the central area where the temples of An and Inanna are, I created the rest of the city using archaeological data where possible and otherwise extrapolating from earlier and later eras at Uruk and other Bronze Age cities.

Three different chronologies have been proposed and are in use for dating Mesopotamian artifacts and events. I have assumed Gilgamesh lived during the Early Dynastic II period, sometime between 2800 and 2700 BCE. Arguments can be made that Gilgamesh lived earlier or later or not at all.

I have also assumed in Gilgamesh's time, the role of king and the role of high (*en*) priest of Inanna belonged to different people.

The Euphrates River (*Buranun*) is more a network of rivers than a single stream. It has changed its course and configuration drastically many times, making the exact position of Uruk relative to the river at the time of Gilgamesh a mystery. Based on hints in ancient texts and startling recent research by German archaeologists using satellite imaging and magnetometry, I have assumed one or another branch of the Euphrates ran *through* Uruk and people traveled about the city both on foot and by boat on a network of canals.

Mesopotamian words. I used the familiar Babylonian names for Gilgamesh, Enkidu, Shamhat, Utnapishtim, and Uruk, following Stephen Mitchell's rendering of Sîn-lēqi-unninni's version of the epic, but I used Sumerian names for gods. Personal names are real Sumerian names or are based on real Sumerian names, but often from later eras because of sparse knowledge of names during Gilgamesh's time. I removed hyphens and accent marks from some names to make them less intimidating.

It may make it easier to keep the long names straight if you remember they are actually sentences. For example, "Inanna-Ama-Mu" means "Inanna is my mother," and "Nanna-Ur-Sag" means "Nanna (the moon god) is a warrior."

My source for Sumerian words was John A. Halloran's "Sumerian Lexicon, version 3.0," available at various sites on the Internet and in print.

Culture and customs. Although in later times, it was believed the priestesses of Inanna routinely sold their bodies on the temple grounds, the evidence for "sacred prostitutes" is sparse, and evidence that they were required to be chaste is more compelling. In later times, Inanna/Ishtar's statue took part in the Sacred Marriage. In early years, this fertility ritual may have been enacted by a priestess of Inanna and the king, and I have assumed such was the case in Gilgamesh's time.

Ritual was a crucial aspect of Sumerian civilization, helping to mark the passage of the seasons, structure everyday life, and provide meaning. Unfortunately, we have little evidence for what happened during festivals or worship or how individuals expressed devotion privately. Rather than make up something misleading, I've given the people of Uruk far more secular and colorless lives than they actually lived.

The relationship between Gilgamesh and Enkidu in Sîn-lēqi-unninni's version of the Gilgamesh epic may have been obvious to the ancient reader, but is not to the modern one. Clearly, Gilgamesh was obsessed with Enkidu as his other self; clearly they loved each other as brothers. But when the epic states they slept in the same bed and walked about holding hands, it's impossible to know whether this was common behavior for friends at that time or whether the two heroes were lovers as well. I have left the situation ambiguous so that the reader may imagine whatever relationship pleases her or him best.

Shamhat's written hymns are probably an anachronism. Written documents we have from this time are exclusively economic and commercial records and word lists for student scribes. Literary compositions, such as hymns, don't appear in the archaeological record until a little later.

About the Author

Author Photograph David Malueg

Shauna Roberts, Ph.D., first fell in love with the ancient Near East in high school when she read Samuel Noah Kramer's *History Begins at Sumer*. After receiving degrees in anthropology from the University of Pennsylvania (Philadelphia) and Northwestern University (Evanston, Ill.), she worked at *Science* magazine and *The Journal of NIH Research*. Since 1990, she has been a freelance medical and science writer and copyeditor, winning several awards.

She writes science fiction and fantasy as well and has had several short stories published. She is a 2009 graduate of the Clarion Science Fiction & Fantasy Writers' Workshop.

Shauna S. Roberts

She grew up in Beavercreek, Ohio, and currently lives with her husband in Southern California. She enjoys herb gardening, quilting, playing medieval and Renaissance music, and bellydancing.

She loves to hear from readers, and free signed bookplates are available upon request.

Write to her at ShaunaRoberts@ShaunaRoberts.com.

http://www.ShaunaRoberts.com

Resources for Learning More About Ancient Mesopotamia

Note: Some of these books are available in several editions. The references given are for the edition I used while writing *Like Mayflies in a Stream*.

For a quick overview

Hunt, Norman Bancroft. *Historical Atlas of Ancient Mesopotamia*. New York: Checkmark Books, 2004. This overview of Mesopotamian history is copiously illustrated in color and covers the time from 5200 BCE to 651 CE.

Steele, Philip. *Eyewitness Mesopotamia*. New York: DK Publishing, 2007. This children's book is suitable for adults, too, with brightly colored pictures on every page, coverage of a wide range of topics, and several appendices.

Wikipedia articles:
- Uruk: http://en.wikipedia.org/wiki/Uruk
- The alabaster vase of the temple of Inanna: http://en.wikipedia.org/wiki/Warka_Vase
- Sumer: http://en.wikipedia.org/wiki/Sumer

To delve deeper

Bertman, Stephen. *Handbook to Life in Ancient Mesopotamia*. New York: Oxford University Press, 2005. Of the several "everyday life in Mesopotamia" books available, I found this one the most comprehensive.

Bottéro, Jean. *Religion in Ancient Mesopotamia*. Chicago: The University of Chicago Press, 2004. This book talks about the deities of ancient Mesopotamia, beliefs about life and creation, and the practice of religion.

Bottéro, Jean. *The Oldest Cuisine in the World: Cooking in Mesopotamia.* Chicago: The University of Chicago Press, 2004. Bottéro discusses food in ancient Mesopotamia based on ancient accounting records and word lists, archaeological evidence, and tablets from 1600 BCE containing 40 recipes.

Meador, Betty De Shong. *Inanna: Lady of Largest Heart: Poems of the Sumerian High Priestess.* Austin: University of Texas Press, 2000. The world's first known works of literature were written by the priestess Enheduanna about 2300 BCE. This books contains translations of Enheduanna's poems in honor of Inanna and biographical information on Enheduanna and her father, Sargon the Great.

Mitchell, Stephen. *Gilgamesh: A New English Version.* New York: Free Press, 2004. This easy-to-read rendering of the "Epic of Gilgamesh" starts with a great introduction to the epic.

Web sites with pictures:
• "Treasures from the Royal Tombs of Ur": http://www.museum.upenn.edu/new/exhibits/ur/gallery.shtml
• Artifacts looted from the Iraq Museum after the American invasion in 2003:
  http://oi.uchicago.edu/OI/IRAQ/dbfiles/Iraqdatabasehome.htm
• "Iraq's Marsh Arabs in the Garden of Eden": http://www.museum.upenn.edu/new/publications/MarshArabsTour.html (16 Web pages of photographs of modern Mi'dan ["Marsh Arabs"], who live much as the people of ancient Sumer did)

To get a taste of scholarly resources

Bottéro, Jean. *Textes culinaires Mésopotamiens.* Winona Lake, Indiana: Eisenbrauns, 1995. This is the scholarly text (in French) on which Bottéro based *The Oldest Cuisine in the World: Cooking in Mesopotamia.*

Eisenbrauns online bookstore. http://www.eisenbrauns.com. This bookstore specializes in scholarly books and journals related to the ancient Near East and Biblical studies.

Halloran, John A. *Sumerian Lexicon: A Dictionary Guide to the Ancient Sumerian Language*. Los Angeles: Logogram Publishing, 2006. An earlier version of this word list is available free on the Web at http://www.sumerian.org/sumerian.pdf.

Liverani, Mario. Uruk: *The First City*. London: Equinox Publishing, 1998. This history of the rise of cities focuses on their economic underpinnings.

Nissen, Hans J. *The Early History of the Ancient Near East 9000–2000 B.C.* Chicago: University of Chicago Press, 1990. This history draws primarily from archaeological evidence rather than ancient texts.

Pollack, Susan. *Ancient Mesopotamia*. Cambridge, England: Cambridge University Press, 2006. This book discusses the development of cities and states from 5000 to 2100 BCE and includes information on class structure and the roles and lives of women and slaves.

The Pennsylvania Sumerian Dictionary: http://psd.museum.upenn.edu/epsd/nepsd-frame.html. Type an English word into this interactive dictionary and get an English transliteration of the Sumerian and Akkadian word. Click on the transliteration and get a picture of the cuneiform symbol and the history of its use.

Breinigsville, PA USA
06 October 2010
246863BV00001B/16/P